The
Guardians

by John Christopher

The Guardians

by John Christopher

The Macmillan Company

1520607

To Susan, J.P.T.C.

Contents

1

Accidents Happen

The Public Library was in a quiet, gloomy street facing the park. It was joined on to rambling dilapidated buildings which had been council offices but were currently used as a warehouse. The library itself was almost as old—a plaque coming away from the wall told of an opening ceremony in 1978—and crumbling badly. There were several large cracks in the concrete surface, once white, now a dirty gray streaked with black.

The interior was not much better. The artificial light supplementing what little filtered in on this dull April afternoon came not from lumoglobes but from antiquated fluorescent tubes. They flickered and hummed; one was dead and another spasmodically blanked and brightened. The librarian, sitting behind his desk, showed no sign of being aware of this. He was a tall, stooping man with a high, domed forehead and a limp white moustache which he continually fingered.

He was a taciturn man, not talking to borrowers except insofar as was absolutely necessary. Once, a couple of years ago, he had engaged Rob in conversation—that was some months after Rob's mother died. Rob had gone to the library in the first place along with her and then had continued on his own. The librarian had said how he had worked here since leaving school, nearly fifty years earlier, and had told him that in those days he had been one of six assistants. There had even been a project for moving to a new, larger building and taking on more staff. It was four decades since that had been abandoned and now he did everything himself. He was past retiring age but stayed because he wanted to. The council talked of closing the library and pulling the building down; meanwhile, they let things run on.

He talked in a half melancholy, half angry way of the virtual disappearance of reading. In his young days there had been no holovision, it was true, but there had been television. People had still read books. People had been different then; more individual, more inquiring. Rob was the only person under fifty who came to the library.

The librarian had looked at Rob with a hopefulness, a hunger almost, that Rob found alarming and embarrassing. To him the library was associated with memories of his mother. He read books because she had, though not the same sort. Both kinds were about the past, but she had liked love stories with country settings. Rob preferred adventures: excitement and the clash of swords. He had read *The Three Musketeers* and its sequels, *Twenty Years After* and *The Vicomte de Bragelonne,* half a dozen times.

He had responded awkwardly and unwillingly to the librarian's remarks and the old man, discouraged, had returned to his customary silence. On this afternoon he stamped his books and dismissed him with a nod. Rob stayed for a moment in the lobby, looking out. The sky was darker than when he had arrived, threatening heavy rain. It was a short walk to the bus stop but a much longer one at the other end; their home was some distance from the nearest route. The stadium, on the other hand, was as near, and his father's duty shift ended within an hour. He could wait and go home with him in the car.

So instead of going away from the park, he crossed it. It was a poor place. There were unkempt flower beds and battered, sickly looking trees around the edges, budding with unpromising leaves. The rest, apart from the children's playground in one corner and a number of football goal posts, was twenty-five acres of scuffed grass and mud, crossed by half a dozen pitted tarmac paths. It did provide, though, a sense of being free of buildings. From the center one could see, above the lower near skyline, the high-rise blocks that stretched out across the sprawl of Greater London to the distant Green Belt dividing this Conurb from the next.

Half a dozen young children were playing and shouting on the swings and roundabouts. A few people were also walking dogs in the park. There were more in the short road leading to the High Street, and the High Street itself was fairly full. Not just with shoppers, he realized, but with the crowd beginning to come away from the afternoon session of the Games. They seemed reasonably orderly, and there had been no real trouble for several weeks—not since the big riot in February.

Rob turned into Fellowes Road, against the stream. It was not long after that he heard a shout from in front, followed by ragged chanting.

"Greens! Greens!"

There were other confused, indistinguishable cries and he became conscious of a tremor, a change of pace, in the mob of people coming toward him. Someone broke into a run, then others. Rob looked for cover and found none. This was a street of old, terraced houses, doors opening directly on the pavement. It was not far to the intersection with Morris Road, and he made an effort to squeeze through that way. But from one moment to the next the crowd solidified, turning into a struggling, shouting battering ram of humanity that lifted and crushed and carried him away.

He remembered that the program that afternoon had been terraplaning. In this, electrocars raced around the high-banked sides of the arena, running almost to vertical directly under the stands, and were boosted by auxiliary rockets at intervals so that they took off and flew through the air. Accidents were frequent, which was one of the things that made the sport popular with spectators. And enthusiasm was roused to a point that could fan the antagonism always present between the four factions—Blacks, Whites, Greens and Reds—to fury. Greens had been dominant in terraplaning for some time. It might be that there had been an upset, or a particularly bad piece of fouling.

He had neither time nor inclination to think much about this. His face was wedged against a brown overcoat, the cloth rough and fusty smelling. Pressure was increasing and he found it difficult to breathe. He remembered that in the

February riot eight people had been crushed to death, in the one just before Christmas more than twenty. He had a glimpse of a corner of a building and realized they had spilled out into the High Street. There was a crash of metal somewhere, people screaming, the bleep of horns. Pressure relaxed slightly; he could move his arms and one foot touched the ground. Then someone or something tripped him and he fell. Someone trod on his arm, someone else, agonizingly, in the small of his back.

Unless he did something he was finished. He could see, indistinctly, through a man's legs, a car which had been brought to a standstill. He forced a way, getting a couple more kicks before he reached it. Then he slid under—there was just enough clearance—and lay there, numb and bruised, watching the torrent of legs and feet and listening to the wild screams and shouts.

Gradually it slackened and ebbed, and at last he could crawl out and stand up. There were several people in the road lying still, others moving and moaning. Two police copters were on the scene, one parked, the second hovering some distance down the street. There were a man and woman in the car under which he had sheltered; its front wing, he saw, had been bent in by pressure. The woman opened a window and asked Rob if he was all right. Before he could do more than nod, the man had set the car in motion, and it drove away, swerving to avoid bodies and other vehicles. Several cars had been turned over and a couple were in nose-to-nose collision.

A hospital copter arced down over the nearby roofs and more were approaching. Rob went to look for his library books which had been torn from his grasp in the rush. He found one in the gutter at the corner of Fellowes Road, the other ten yards farther up. It was open and had been trodden down: there was a heel mark deeply impressed on one page and another was torn almost across. He pressed it back into shape as best he could, tucked both books under his arm, and headed for the stadium.

The stadium was nearly half a mile long and rose three hundred feet in the air, an oval of dull gold unbroken on the outside. A few people were still coming away from the nearest exit gate and cars were issuing from the below-ground parking places, but the main rush was over. Rob went to a service entrance and showed his disk to the scanner. It was a duplicate which his father had obtained for him; strictly speaking they were only on issue to staff but the rule was not taken seriously. The door hissed open and closed behind him when he had gone through. He turned right along the panel-lit corridor, heading for the main electrical section. He would not be allowed into any of the control rooms, but he could wait in a leisure room.

Before he reached it, though, he saw someone he knew. It was at the point where several corridors intersected and the man crossed just ahead of him. Rob called, and he stopped and waited for him to come up.

It was Mr. Kennealy, a friend of his father, also an electrician. He was a stocky, slow-speaking man with a broad face and very black hair. He never showed much emotion but Rob thought he had an odd look now.

"Did they tell you, then, Rob?"

"Tell me what, Mr. Kennealy? I thought I'd go home with Dad." Mr. Kennealy was studying him and Rob became aware of his dirty and disheveled appearance. "There was a riot over toward the High Street. I had to get under a car. . . ."

"There's been an accident," Mr. Kennealy said quietly.

"To do with . . . ?"

He did not want to finish the sentence. Apprehension made his throat dry.

"They've taken your father to the hospital, Rob. He got hold of a live wire by mistake. He was pretty badly shocked before anyone could switch off."

"He's not . . ."

"No. But he'll be away for a while. I was wondering how to get a message to you. I think you'd better stay with us for the time being."

They lived in a high rise overlooking the stadium and only a few minutes' walk away. He had been there many times with his father and liked Mrs. Kennealy, a large, red-faced woman, strong armed and heavy handed. It was much better than the thought of going back on his own to the empty apartment.

"Can I go to see him in hospital?"

"Not today. There's visiting tomorrow afternoon." Mr. Kennealy glanced at his finger-watch. "Come on. I'll take you back. I can clock off early for once."

They walked over in silence: Mr. Kennealy did not say anything and Rob was not eager to talk either. He was not only shocked by what had happened but confused. His father had got hold of a live wire . . . but he had always been so careful, checking and double-checking everything. He wanted to ask Mr. Kennealy about it, but he felt that to do so would be a sort of criticism.

Two of the three lifts in the block were out of order and they had to wait some time to be taken up. Mr. Kennealy complained of this to his wife, who came out of the kitchenette as they went into the tiny hall of the apartment. Maintenance was terrible and getting worse.

"You'll have to look at the HV, too," Mrs. Kennealy added. "It's gone wrong again. You're back early. I see you've got Rob with you. Is Jack coming up later?"

He told her briefly what had happened. She came to Rob, put an arm across his shoulders and gave him a squeeze. He was aware of looks passing between them which he could not read, and was not sure he would have wanted to.

"I've got the kettle on. Go and sit down, the pair of you, and I'll bring you some tea."

In the sitting room the holovision set was blaring away, showing a soap opera. The figures were hazy, occasionally switching from three- to two-dimensional, and the colors were peculiar. Mr. Kennealy cursed and, after switching off, removed the back and started tinkering. Rob watched him for a time and then went to the kitchenette. There was barely room for anyone else when Mrs. Kennealy was there.

"What is it then, Rob?" she asked.

"I was wondering if there was anything I could mend this book with. There's a page torn."

"Books." She shook her head. "What do you want with them, anyway? Well, I suppose it takes all sorts. There's some sticky tape somewhere. Yes, on that top shelf."

Rob put the torn edges together and carefully taped them. Watching him, she asked him how it had got in such a state, and he told her about the riot.

"Hooligans. There's too much of it altogether," she said. "They ought to put them in the army and send them out to China."

The war in China had been going on as long as he could remember. Troublemakers were sometimes given the option of enlisting and going out there instead of to prison. It was all far away and unreal. She had said it perfunctorily, her mind more on making the tea. Now she gave him a tray, with teapot and cups and saucers and a plate of chocolate biscuits.

"Take this through while I wipe up," she told him. "I'll be along in a minute."

Mr. Kennealy was still fiddling with the inside of the HV set. Rob put the tray down on a coffee table and went over to the window. The long-threatened rain had come and was sheeting down the chasm between this block and the next to the dark gloomy street hundreds of feet below. He stood watching it, thinking of his father and feeling miserable.

The apartment had a spare bedroom, once used by the Kennealys' daughter, who had married and left home. Rob was put up there, in a pink bed patterned with roses. He read for a time and then, tired, thumbed out the light and was soon asleep.

He woke again, feeling thirsty, and made for the bathroom to get a drink of water. He went very quietly, imagining it was the middle of the night and not wanting to dis-

turb anyone, but heard voices as he crossed the lobby and
noticed a line of light under the sitting-room door. Men's
voices, three at least. They seemed to be arguing about
something. Coming back quietly from the bathroom he
heard his father's name mentioned, and stopped to listen.
He could only catch a word here or there—not enough to
get the sense of what was being said. He realized how bad
it would look if someone were to come out and find him
eavesdropping, and went back to bed.

He did not sleep, though. He could hear the low murmur
of voices through the wall and found that he was straining
to listen to them. Then after what seemed a long time there
was the sound of a door opening, and the voices louder and
clearer in the lobby outside.

A man said: "There's something wrong. I told him a
week ago he needed to watch out."

"Accidents happen," another voice said.

"You can't take chances," the first voice insisted. "I'd
warned him. You have to take account of the risks. This is
a dangerous business. We'd all better remember that. Not
just for ourselves but for the others, too."

"Quiet," Mr. Kennealy said. "The boy's in there. And
the door's ajar."

There were footsteps and the door was gently shut. Rob
heard their muted voices for a few more moments before the two visitors took their leave and Mr. Kennealy
went to his bedroom. Rob lay awake still, thinking about
what he had heard. He was angry at the things the men had
said, the first speaker anyway. He was not only blaming his
father for what had happened, but suggesting that he had

put others at risk. How could that be true, when it was just
a matter of touching a wire that was live when he thought
it was insulated?

And Mr. Kennealy . . . he had stopped the man, but
only because he had thought Rob might hear. He had not
stood up for his father as he ought to have done. Rob was
hating him, too, as he finally fell asleep.

The hospital was a fairly new building, more than forty
floors high, its exterior in pale-green plastibrick with ano-
dized aluminum trim on the windows. The windows
gleamed brightly in spring sunshine—the sky was blue except for a few white clouds in the west. At the very top was
the balcony ringing the roof garden and heliport, toward
which an ambulance copter was at this moment dropping.
The doctors also parked their copters up there, coming in
from the County, but there would be few at present. Only
a skeleton staff remained on duty on Sunday.

The Kennealys and Rob joined the queue of people waiting for the lifts, which did not operate until the start of
visiting hour. At least, this being a hospital, they were all
working. They were whisked up quickly and into a second
line of people waiting outside the ward door. A bored medi-
cal clerk, his head tonsured in the latest fashion, checked off
names on a list. When they reached him, he said, "Randall?
Not down here. You must have come to the wrong ward."

"We were told F.17."

"They're always getting things wrong," the clerk said in-
differently. "You'd better go and ask downstairs."

Mr. Kennealy said in a quiet but hard voice, "No, you

call them up. We're not wasting time going all the way down there again on your say-so."

"The procedure . . ."

Mr. Kennealy leaned over the desk. "Never mind the procedure," he said. "You call them."

The clerk obeyed sullenly. He did not use the visiphone but his handphone. They heard but could not make out the tinny whisper of speech at the other end. The clerk asked for a check on Randall, J., admitted the previous afternoon. He said: "Yes, got that," and replaced the phone.

"Well," Mr. Kennealy said, "where is he?"

"In the morgue," the clerk said. "He was taken into Intensive Care this morning and died of heart failure."

"That's impossible!" Mr. Kennealy said.

His face was white, Rob saw, while the shock hit him too. The clerk shrugged. "Death's never impossible. They'll give you particulars at the office. Next, please."

Mrs. Kennealy came with Rob to help sort things out. She clucked over the untidiness and set about putting the place to rights while Rob packed his clothes and belongings. The furniture, he supposed, would be sold. He wondered if it would be possible to keep the saddle-backed chair in which his mother used to sit in the evenings. He would have to ask Mrs. Kennealy if she could find room for it, but did not want to bother her at the moment.

He left her cleaning and rearranging the living room and went into his father's bedroom. The bed was made, but a towel had been left lying carelessly across the foot, and two bedroom slippers were at opposite ends of the rug. There was a half-empty pack of cigarettes on the bedside table, a glass with a little water in it, and the miniradio which his father had sometimes listened to at night. He remembered waking and hearing the sound of music through the dividing wall.

He still could not properly grasp what had happened. The suddenness was as shocking as the fact. His mother had been continuously ill for a long time before she died—he could scarcely remember a time when she was not ill. Her death had been no less horrifying for that, but even then, when he was ten, he had known it to be inevitable. His father, on the other hand, had been a strong, active man, always in good health. It was impossible to imagine him dead. He could not be.

Rob opened the wardrobe. The clothes would probably be sold, too—they would fit Mr. Kennealy. He felt his eyes sting, and pulled open one of the drawers at the bottom. More clothes. A second drawer. Folded pullovers, and a cardboard box. On the outside was written "Jenny," his mother's name. He took it out and opened it.

The first thing he saw was her photograph. He had not known one existed: he remembered his father once trying to get her to have a photograph taken, and her refusal. This was an old-fashioned 2-D print, and it showed her as much younger than he had known her—scarcely more than twenty, with brown hair down her shoulders instead of short as she had worn it in later years.

He looked at it for a long time, trying to read behind the slight, anxious smile on her face. Then he heard Mrs. Kennealy calling him. He had time to see that there were other things in the box—a curl of hair in a transparent locket, letters in a bundle held together by a rubber band. He closed the box and put it with his own things before going to see what Mrs. Kennealy wanted.

Rob was called from geography to the principal's office. They were without a master at the time, though of course under closed-circuit TV observation at the main switchboard; and the holovision set was taking them on a conducted tour of Australia, with a bouncing, breezy commentary full of not very funny little jokes. The voice blanked out though vision continued, and with a warning ping a voice said, "Randall. Report to the principal immediately. Repeat. Randall to the principal's office."

The commentary came up again. One or two of the boys made their own even less funny jokes about possible reasons for his being summoned, but Mr. Spennals was on the switchboard that morning and the majority kept their attention firmly on the screen; he was not a man to trifle with.

Assemblies apart, Rob had seen the principal twice before; once when he joined the school, the second time when they met in a corridor and he was given a message to deliver to the masters' common-room. He looked at Rob now as though wondering who he was. This was not surprising since there were nearly two thousand boys in the school. He said, "Randall," tentatively, and then more firmly, "Randall, this is Mr. Chalmers from the Education Office."

The second man was broad where the principal was thin, with hairy cheeks and a quiet watchful expression. Rob said, "Good morning, sir," to him, and he nodded but made no reply.

"Mr. Chalmers has been looking into your case, following the regrettable death of your father," the principal said. "You have only one close relative, I understand, an aunt living in"—he glanced at a pad in front of him—"in the Sheffield Conurb. She has been consulted. I'm afraid she does not feel able to offer you a home. There are difficulties—her husband is in poor health. . . ."

Rob said nothing. It had not occurred to him that this would even be suggested. The principal continued, "Under the circumstances it is felt that the best solution to your problem—in fact the only solution—will be to have you transferred to a boarding school where you can have full care and attention. We feel . . ."

Rob was so surprised that he interrupted. "Can't I stay with the Kennealys, sir?"

"The Kennealys?" The two men looked at each other. "Who are they?"

Rob explained. The principal said:

"Yes, I see. The neighbors who have been looking after you. But that would not be suitable, of course, for the longer term."

"But they have a spare room, sir."

"Not suitable," the principal repeated in a flat, authoritative voice. "You will be transferred to the Barnes Boarding School. You are excused classes for the remainder of the day. Transport will be sent to pick you up at nine o'clock tomorrow morning."

Rob took the bus to the stadium where he knew Mr. Kennealy was on duty. On the way he thought about the State boarding schools. Some were supposed to be not quite so bad as others, but they were all regarded with a mixture of contempt and dread. They catered to orphans and the children of broken marriages, but also to certain types of juvenile delinquents. There were ugly rumors about the life there, particularly about the terrible food and the discipline.

Rob sent in a message asking for Mr. Kennealy, who came out to the leisure room ten minutes later. Rob had been watching the closed-circuit holovision which showed what was happening in the arena. It was gladiators in high-wire combat. In this, men fought with light, blunt-ended fiberglass spears from separate wires that approached each other at differing heights and distances. The wire system was complex and changed during the contest. The drop could be into water or onto firm ground, which in this case was covered with artificial thorn bushes, glinting with murderous-looking spikes. A loser always got hurt, sometimes badly, occasionally fatally. There were three men in the present fight and one had already fallen and limped away with difficulty. The remaining two swayed and probed at each other in the bluish light cast by the weather screen which at the moment covered the top of the stadium.

"Well, Rob, what are you doing away from school?" Mr. Kennealy asked.

Rob told him what had happened. Mr. Kennealy listened in silence.

"They said I couldn't stay with you, but it's not true, is it?"

Mr. Kennealy replied heavily, "If that's what the regulations say, there's nothing we can do."

"But you could go and see them—you could apply for me."

"It wouldn't do any good."

"There was a boy at school last year—Jimmy McKay. His mother went off and his father couldn't manage. He went to Mrs. Pearson in your block and he's still living there."

"The Pearsons may have adopted him."

"Couldn't you? Adopt me, that is?"

"Not without your aunt giving consent."

"Well, she won't have me herself. She's said so."

"That doesn't mean she'd be ready to sign you away. She might be thinking things will change later, that she can take you then."

"They could ask her, couldn't they? I'm pretty sure she'd say yes."

"It's not as easy as that." Mr. Kennealy paused and Rob waited for him to go on. "What I mean is, this may be the best thing for you. You'll be safer there."

"Safer? How?"

Mr. Kennealy started to say something, then shook his head.

"Better looked after. And with boys of your own age. Mrs. Kennealy and I are too old for a boy like you to have to live with."

"You said 'safer.'"

"It was a slip of the tongue."

There was a silence. Mr. Kennealy was not meeting Rob's eyes. Rob felt he could see the truth of the matter. All these were excuses, attempts to conceal the central fact: the Kennealys did not want him. He felt a bit as he had when Mr.

Kennealy had not spoken up for his father against the man who had said that he was to blame for getting killed, but now it was more a feeling of desolation than anger.

"Yes, Mr. Kennealy," Rob said.

He had turned away. He found himself grasped by the shoulders, and Mr. Kennealy stared into his eyes.

"It's for your good, Rob," he said. "Believe that. I can't explain, but it's for your good."

Inside the holovision screen one figure lunged, the other parried and struck back and the first dropped ludicrously on his back, into the thorns. Rob nodded. "I'd better go back and see about packing my things."

2

A Disgrace to This House

The boarding school stood on land enclosed by a bend in the River Thames. The main part, including the games area and most of the classrooms, was in late twentieth century style, bare and sprawling. The boarding houses which marched along the inner perimeter were more recent, austere within but their exteriors colored and ornamented. Rob had been allotted to G-House, which was pastel blue crossed by broad transverse stripes of orange.

For the first few days he was too confused to take in much beyond an impression of constant activity. The day was filled to overflowing. Broadcast alarms woke the dormitories at half past six and there was a scramble to wash and dress and reach the games area by seven. They were nearly a quarter of a mile from it—only H-House was farther off. You had to run in wet weather, with a cape flapping around you. On arrival there was roll call. Latecomers, if only by half a minute, were put on report and given extra gymnastics in the evening.

The half hour of exercises in the morning was theoretically followed by half an hour's free time before breakfast at eight o'clock. But you quickly learned the importance of queuing in advance outside the dining room because the food, apart from being poor and badly cooked, was never sufficient to go round. For those at the end of the queue the horrible lumpy porridge was further diluted with hot water, there was half a portion of reconstituted egg or half a rissole, and there might not even be a slice of bread. Senior boys pushed their way to the front at the last minute; juniors had no option but to stand in line.

Morning school was from 8:45 till 12:30, when there was a break for lunch and more queuing. In the afternoons they had games—gymnastics again, in bad weather—until tea at half past four. Then there was evening school from five to seven, after which you were free until lights out at nine. Free, that is, if you had not been detailed for extra gym, or for one of the hundred jobs which prefects or any other seniors required to have done. Rob went to bed exhausted each night and slept soundly on a lumpy three-section mattress resting on the metal slats of his truckle bed.

Gradually he took stock of his surroundings. There were thirty boys of roughly his own age in his dormitory. He was aware of something going on at the far end on the first night, of voices and cries of pain, but he was too tired to pay much attention. It happened the next night, and he realized that there were bigger boys present and that one of the younger boys was being tormented. D'Artagnan, he thought, would not have lain quietly in bed. He would have done something—tackled the bullies. Nor was it much good putting up the excuse that he had no Porthos, Athos or Aramis, and no prospect of finding them among the unfriendly jostling boys in the dormitory. D'Artagnan would have acted on his own. The tormentors left in the end. He could hear the boy sobbing after they had gone, and fell asleep with the sound in his ears.

He asked a ginger-haired, pale boy called Perkins about it the following day while they were waiting to go into class.

"Simmons, you mean? He was just getting the Routine."

"The Routine?"

Perkins explained: it was a ritual bullying conducted on new boys.

"I'm new, and they haven't done anything to me," Rob said.

"Too new. The first three weeks they leave you alone. You've got your turn to come."

"What do they do? What did they do to you?"

"Various things," Perkins said. "The worst was tying string around my forehead and tightening it. I thought my eyes were going to pop out."

"Did it hurt a lot?"

"Did it hurt! I'll give you a tip: yell just a bit. If you don't yell they keep at you till you do. And if you yell too much they keep on as well. If it's just a bit, they get bored."

They went into class—history of engineering. The master was a small, neat, gray-haired man who rattled through his talk quickly and perfunctorily. He was dealing with rocket

propulsion, flashing slide after slide through the pro-
jector. He asked for questions in a way that did not invite
response, but Rob said, "It's not much used now, is it,
sir?"

The master looked at him with some surprise. "Hardly
at all. In terraplaning, of course, but there are no really
useful applications."

"It was chiefly intended for interplanetary exploration,
wasn't it, sir?"

"Yes."

"Why was that given up? Men landed on the moon, and
probes reached Mars."

The master paused before replying. "It was stopped because it was pointless, Randall. It is Randall? Billions of
pounds were spent on utterly useless projects. We have different priorities now. Our aims are the happiness and well-
being of mankind. We live in a saner, more ordered world
than our fathers did. Now, if you have satisfied your vanity
by interrupting, we will get on with the lesson. A much
more useful invention, and one that is still used in an improved form, is the jet engine. The origin of this . . ."

Some of the other boys were looking at him with disgust.
In his old school it had not been popular to ask questions.
He realized it was probably going to be worse here.

He wondered if the world really was so much happier
than in the past. No one starved, it was true, and the only
war was the faraway one in China. No one who stayed out
of trouble had to fight in that if they did not want to. There
were holovision and the Games, the carnivals—all kinds of
amusements. Riots, too, of course, but they were over

quickly and mostly people could avoid them. Many seemed to enjoy them. What the master had said was probably right.

Rob came back to more immediate considerations and thought about what Perkins had told him. It was a consolation that they left you alone for three weeks. He had only been here three days.

The weather had been blustering and rainy when Rob first came to the boarding school. Then there were several days of warm, bright weather, more like summer than spring. On the evening of the second he succeeded in dodging a group of prefects on the prowl for slaves and made his way around the edge of the playing fields—crossing them was probably forbidden and anyway would have been conspicuous—to the river.

It surprised him that no one had done the same. This might be forbidden too, but he was prepared to chance that to get an hour's peace and solitude. It was also true, as he had learned long ago, that most people—boys or adults—disliked being alone. He was glad of his own company normally, at present very much so.

He had brought a book with him and, on impulse, his mother's photograph and the bundle of letters. The book was one of the two he had borrowed from the Public Library. He had not had time to take it back before leaving the Kennealys and he did not see how he was going to be able to return it now. The library was six or seven miles away and, in any case, boys were not allowed out of the school grounds without special permission—never granted to a junior. He supposed he would have to hand the books in for the school to send back.

But he was not in a hurry to do this because as far as he could see they were irreplaceable. There was no library in the school, no books except those used as aids to the various visual learning techniques. He had not really thought there would be, but it was a blow all the same. He was reading the books he had as slowly as possible, drawing them out. This one was called *The Napoleon of Notting Hill* and was about a Victorian London in which armies of local patriots fought pitched battles in the gaslit streets. It was fantasy, of course. Even a hundred and fifty years ago London had been enough of a Conurb for that to have been impossible. But it was nice to think about. He thought of the struggles today between supporters of the different terraplane factions. It was not the same. A parish would have been something worth fighting for. He read half a dozen pages and closed the volume at the end of a chapter.

He looked at the photograph instead and wondered about the smile. He had known his mother as someone not only ill, but also unhappy. She had a few acquaintances, no friends. Rob held the bundle of letters in his hands. Their very existence was a link with the past. No one wrote letters nowadays. If people did not visiphone, they sent sound-grams. It was strange, and strangely pleasant, to think of one person writing words on paper, slowly and carefully, to send to another.

He had thought before of reading them but had held back. They were private: probably he should have got rid of them, dropped them in the nearest waste-disposer. He pulled off the rubber band and held the top envelope in his hands. They were both dead, and he was left. He pulled the sheets of paper out carefully, unfolded them and began to read.

They were love letters as he had expected. It was not on that account he wanted to read them. The thought had been that he might somehow get closer to the memory of his mother, understand the smile in the photograph. The letter did not help though. It was conventional, telling the man how much she loved him, how slow the days were passing before she could hope to see him again. Rob felt some disappointment. He was folding the letter up to put it back in the envelope when something struck him. The address at the top: White Cottage, Shearam, Glos. "Glos." was short for Gloucestershire. And Gloucestershire was in the County.

He looked through other letters which confirmed it. His mother had been born in the County. She had met his father when he came in to work on a special job—there must have been contact still in those days—had fallen in love with him and come to the Conurb to marry him.

The County was not mentioned on holovision, but Rob had heard talk about it. The tone was usually a mixture of envy and contempt. The gentry lived in the County, the gentry and their servants. There were others, the Commuters, who worked professionally in the Conurbs but had their permanent homes in the County. Doctors, lawyers, senior officials, factory executives came into this class. Some went back nightly by private copter, others on weekends.

Those who lived all the time in the Conurbs had no desire to cross the border to the other world. There were good reasons for this. Life in the County was supposed to be very dull. There were no Games there and no holovision. No cities—no dance halls or amusement parks, no bright lights. Nothing but fields and villages and a few very small towns. Horses, seen in the Conurbs only at race tracks, provided the universal means of transport. (Copters were only used by Commuters to get in and out.) Everything was slow, unhurried, boring. There were no electrocars or buses, no monorail trains.

Worse than anything was the fact that there was, as Conurbans understood it, no community life. There were no crowds, no sense of being part of a noisy mass of people who could give each other reassurance and security. Conurbans were sociable and gregarious, enjoying one another's company. At the seaside the really popular beaches were those where everyone was packed together, the sand barely visible for the bodies lying or sitting on it. In the County, they knew, there were empty fields stretching to the horizon, shores on which the only sound was the cry of gulls, moors where a man might walk—horrifying thought—for hours and meet no one.

Rob had heard these defects dwelt on. The gentry were probably used to them. They lived idly on their investments rather than working. That might be enviable (though the working week in the Conurbs was only twenty hours) but not what went with it. The gentry's lives were dull because they themselves were only half alive. They could not have put up with the excitement, the "go," which characterized life in the Conurbs. As for the Commuters, they might be bosses but they were really no better than hangers-on, aping their betters. There was something sneaky and dishonest about living in two worlds. The Conurbans prided themselves on their own single-heartedness.

Views such as these were well known to Rob, though he recalled now that he had never heard them expressed by his parents. He had not challenged them, though he had not in every way agreed with them. There was even something desirable in the thought of those empty fields, the unpeopled moors and beaches. But he had kept his feelings to himself.

One other thing he remembered. The greatest contempt had been reserved for those who lived in the County as servants, ministering to the needs of the gentry. Their spinelessness in accepting that kind of servitude was seen as utterly repulsive. He realized why the County had never been mentioned by his mother and father. His mother obviously had not been gentry, so she must have come from the servant class.

It was a shock, a great shock. He felt ashamed and then, in an odd way, angry. His mother had not been spineless. Gentle, yes, but brave also, especially during the final years of illness. If they were wrong about that they could be wrong about other things, too. He realized with another smaller shock that he was thinking of the other Conurbans as Them—something different from himself.

There were no lessons on Saturday morning but that did not make the day one to look forward to, because instead there was the weekly school inspection. Friday evening was devoted to an extensive cleaning and tidying program, supervised by the prefects, and this was continued after breakfast on Saturday. The inspection, by the Master of Discipline, started at eleven and lasted for roughly an hour and a half. He took with him an entourage of prefects, who noted down the names of offenders against his rules for later punishment.

On the first Saturday inspection Rob had been checked for an untidy bed but let off, as a new arrival, with a warning to do better in future. The three sections of the mattress had to be stacked, one above the other and perfectly aligned at the head of the bed, and various items of clothing and belongings—best jacket, spare shoes, toilet articles, sports kit and so on—had to be set out on top of them in a particular order. On the lower part of the bed blankets were placed, folded to a certain size, with the following week's sheets and pillowslip. All other belongings had to be disposed of neatly in the locker beside the bed.

The second week he was kept busy on Friday in the work gang that was detailed to scrub the dormitory floor and polish the taps and other fittings in the washroom. In the morning, immediately after breakfast, he was detailed to a party picking up scraps of paper all around G-House. He was not released until half past ten and sprinted along with the others to get on with the job of tidying his own bed space. But he was caught on the way upstairs by a senior boy and made to help in laying out his things. He did it badly and was made to do it again. It was eleven before he was dismissed.

Everyone else's bed was ready. There was still time

though, he thought as he feverishly set about his task. On the previous Saturday the inspecting party had not reached them until after twelve. He folded the blankets, saw they would not do, and tried again. The second effort was worse than the first. His fingers by this time were thumbs. He did it once more; better, but the edges were not exactly in line. He was forced to start all over.

The other boys were playing dice and talking. Then one who had been posted as a lookout at the top of the stairs called: "Stand by your beds! They're here and coming up."

Rob somehow managed to finish putting the specified articles on show. Some of his other things were on the shelf which ran along the wall above the beds. This had to be clean for Saturday inspection. He grabbed everything and bundled it into the locker, closed and latched it, and stood to attention by his bed as the Master of Discipline and the prefects came into the dormitory at the far end.

Only one boy was checked, for a missing toothbrush, as they made their way along the line. There was an encouraging atmosphere of good humor: the master cracked a joke and all the prefects laughed at it. Two beds from Rob, the master paused to offer a word of commendation. "Very good. A neat effort." He passed the next bed with a cursory glance and stood in front of Rob's.

He was a small man, shorter than any of the prefects, meticulous in appearance with a strong, closely trimmed black beard. He stood with hands folded behind his back, head thrust forward. He gave a small nod, which Rob thought meant his bed had passed muster. Then he said quietly:

"You are the new boy. I saw you last week. I remember telling you your blankets were not properly squared."

"Yes, sir."

"They still aren't, are they?" He reached forward with a small silver-topped walking stick, pointing to them. "If anything they're worse."

The stick pointed to the shoes.

"Also untidy. Sides should be touching, toe points level." The tip of the stick flipped a shoe over. "And what's this? Insteps not polished? You know the rules: both insteps and uppers of spare shoes to be polished to a high gloss. Well?"

"I didn't have time, sir."

"Time! You've been here over a week." He stared at Rob. "Name, boy."

"Randall, sir."

Rob watched in resignation as the prefect spoke into his soundpad. At any rate it was over and they would move on. But they did not. The master said, "Randall, I have a feeling about you. I have a feeling that you are an idle and untidy boy. Let me tell you that neither of those qualities will be tolerated in this school. Is that clear?"

"Yes, sir."

Cold, blue eyes studied him. He must go now, Rob thought. But instead he said, "Open your locker."

"Sir, I wasn't able . . ."

"Open it, Randall." Rob undid the catch and opened the door. "Stand aside."

It looked worse than he had expected: objects heaped and bundled together in confusion. In a voice still calm, the master said, "This is disgraceful. Completely disgraceful."

He stepped forward and hooked with his stick, bringing everything cascading onto the floor.

"Disgraceful," he repeated. He poked the stick in. "And what's this? What's this, Randall?"

"A book, sir."

"Not one but two. Are books among the items permitted to be kept in lockers?"

"I don't know, sir."

"So you have not made yourself familiar with school regulations?"

"They're library books, sir. I meant to . . ."

"Library books," the master said. He prodded one contemptuously. "Objects which have been passed from hand to unwashed hand. Filty unsanitary things. Traps for germs. You disgust me, Randall." The calmness had gone and his voice was hard and angry. "You are a disgrace to this house and to the school. Bentley!"

The perfect with the soundpad said, "Sir?"

"See that these things are removed and burned."

"But, sir," Rob interrupted. "The library . . ."

The blue eyes stared at him. "A disgrace. I trust your school fellows will be as ashamed of you as I am. And I hope they make their feelings plain. Pick up the rest of your things and tidy them."

He had to report to the prefects' room immediately after lunch and there was given his punishment. He was on extra duties every evening for the next month. Bentley told him this coldly and turned away as he dismissed him. The boys in the dormitory had already taken their cue from the Master of Discipline: no one was speaking to him. When he met Perkins on the stairs the ginger-haired boy went past him as though he did not exist.

It was unpleasant, but perhaps less so for him than it would have been for others since he had never fully shared the overwhelming Conurban need to be an accepted member of the group. It might not be easy to grin at it, but he could hope to bear it. His first stint of penal labor came that evening. It was the pointless task of picking up all the loose stones he could find in the vicinity of the house and stacking them in a particular place. He was warned that he would be under observation from the window of the prefects' room and that he had better put his back into it. The job was tiring as well as boring. When the bell rang for bedtime he felt utterly exhausted. He undressed, washed and brushed his teeth, and climbed into bed as the lights went out. He could sleep and forget things for a few hours.

The noise of feet at the far end of the dormitory came as he was drifting into sleep. He realized vaguely what it must be—senior boys out on the Routine. Not coming for him: he was still a long way short of the three weeks' grace new boys were given. He thought of D'Artagnan again but was even less moved to follow his example. He had enough troubles of his own. Then footsteps approached and lights flashed in his eyes. He sat up.

Two of them had torches, another a portable lumoglobe which he put on top of Rob's locker. There were seven or eight; it was difficult to be sure in the semidarkness.

One said: "You're a disgrace, Randall. Isn't that true?"

They were probably on their way to some victim. If he humored them they might go on.

"Yes," he said.

"Yes, what?"

"Yes, sir."

"That's better. Repeat after me: 'I know I am a disgrace and I am ashamed of myself.' "

Rob repeated the words mechanically.

The boy continued, "I ask the house for punishment because I know I deserve it."

"I've been punished," Rob said. "A month of extra duties."

"Not enough. Not enough for bringing dirty, germy books into the house. And that was school punishment, anyway. What you need is house punishment. Isn't it?" Rob did not reply. "Dumb insolence. That makes it worse. Looks as though he needs the Routine. A special routine."

There was no point, Rob thought, in saying anything. He stared up silently at the faces that surrounded his bed.

"On the other hand you're not supposed to get the routine till you've been here three weeks. And you've admitted you're ashamed of yourself. We might let things go for the time being. Just show you really are ashamed, really sorry for being so disgusting. Get out of bed and get down and kiss our feet. Starting with mine."

He still stared at them. His tormentor said, "What about it, Randall?"

Rob shook his head. "No."

"You're going to regret that. All right. We apply the Routine."

Rob struggled but they pinioned him quite easily. Their faces grinned at him, ugly in the light from the lumoglobe. One said, "The hammer? Knock a bit of decency into him?"

They liked the idea. The hammer that was produced was not very big and the head was not metal but hard rubber. It was swung in front of his face for some moments and then tapped, fairly sharply, against his forehead. The feeling was more unpleasant than painful. The tapping went on in a steady rhythm. After a time it began to hurt. He winced, and one of them said, "We seem to be getting through. Ready to kiss our feet yet?" He shook his head and the hammer landed in a different place. "We'd better keep on, then."

Soon it was hurting a lot. He remembered Perkins's advice to yell a bit, but he could not bring himself to do it any more than he could have gone down on his knees to them. He gritted his teeth and turned his head slightly. The hammer hit him in another place, a small relief but one that did not last.

The pain was one big ache with smaller sharper jabs exploding into it. He was less aware of the voices and faces. His mind concentrated on the hurt. It went on and on, a savage unending nightmare. He thought he was going to faint and hoped he would, but the pain drew him back. In the end, involuntarily, he cried out, in a scream of agony. The tapping stopped.

Someone said, "O.K. for now. We'll carry on the treatment tomorrow night."

The lumoglobe was picked up. The voices and footsteps went away down the dormitory. Rob's head ached violently. Sleep was far away. Tomorrow night . . . And the night after? Once they started there seemed no reason why they should ever stop.

He tried to think objectively, though the ache in his head made that difficult. He would be here until school-leaving age, seventeen. Four years. Even if the bullying stopped there were all the other things. No home to go back to, no privacy, no books. The place was bad enough in itself: to get used to it would be even worse. Better being tortured than turning into something like the torturers.

But if he managed to get away, where could he go? His aunt—the Sheffield Conurb was a long way off and there was no reason to think she would help him. The Kennealys were nearer. But there was no hope there, either. If Mr. Kennealy had not been willing to have him before, he would certainly not do so when it would involve trouble with the authorities over someone who had run away from a State Boarding School.

What else? Try and live on his own somehow? But how? It might be possible to dodge the police for a week or two, sleeping in the open or in derelict houses, but he could not do that for long. The little money he had would quickly run out, and there would be no way of getting more except by joining one of the criminal gangs of the underworld. And they probably wouldn't want him either.

One could not hide among the crowds of ordinary people. Everyone had a particular place in society, a routine by which he could be identified. There was no concealment in the teeming streets of the Conurbs. It was hopeless to imagine it.

The Conurbs . . . He sat up in bed, and his head hurt

still more. The idea was shocking, unthinkable by the standards of the world he knew, but at the same time exciting. His mother had come from the County to the Conurb. Was it possible—dare he think of reversing the process? Those empty fields. Farmlands. Surely there would be food among farmlands?

He lay back and thought about it, thought very hard.

3

The Man with the Rabbits

On Sunday mornings breakfast was not until eight thirty
and there were no morning gymnastics. The alarm bell rang
an hour before that. After breakfast boys returned to their
houses and concentrated on smartening themselves up for
chapel at ten. The service lasted an hour and a half, and was
followed by a free hour before lunch.

During lunch, Rob had decided, would be the best time
for making a break. There was much less chance of being
observed—Sunday lunch was the only halfway tolerable
meal of the week and no one, certainly none of the prefects,
was likely to miss it. If his absence were noticed afterward it
would probably be assumed that he was hiding to dodge the
extra work he would otherwise be landed for in the afternoon. Not until the evening roll call would he be identified
as absent. That gave him more than six hours to get clear.

When the lunch bell rang he doubled back to the house. All the boys had small cases to be used on rarely granted visits to relations, and Rob packed what he wanted to take— his mother's letters and photograph, extra clothes, toilet articles, a bar of chocolate he had saved—in this. Then he headed for the main gate, taking the path at the back of the boarding houses where there was less likelihood of being seen.

Once outside he walked quickly down the long road leading to the bus route. He was lucky: a bus came within minutes, gliding into the bay on the power beam from the underground electric cable. He dropped his coin in the slot and went through to the back. There were not more than half a dozen other passengers.

The morning had been cloudy but the sun now broke clear and was hot through the glass windows. The streets carried little traffic—most people would have gone out of London for the day to one of the recreation areas, perhaps to the seaside on the promise of fine weather, to return in the evening untroubled to their homes. Rob felt depressed. He had been carried this far on a wave of determination and planning, but with nothing to do but watch the city's streets pass by, doubts came. He would never make it. They would pick him up long before he reached the border and take him back to school. And then? Heavier punishment, he supposed, official and unofficial, and the added humiliation of having to wear a wrist transmitter continually broadcasting his position to the control panel in the main office. There would be no second chance of escape.

There was the argument that he ought to get off the bus

and catch the next one back, hope to sneak in again without being seen. There was another, though—that he must make sure they did not catch him. The bus circled Trafalgar Square, with the pigeons walking about in the sunshine, the fountains flashing, Nelson looking down from the top of the plexiglass pillar which had replaced the original stone one. No, Rob decided, he was not going back. And he was not going to get caught.

The bus drew up at the Monorail Terminus and he got out. In a visiphone booth, checking the mirror to see that no one was watching him, he slipped off his school blazer with its bright-red trim and distinctive badge and rolled it up. Then he went out and stuffed it between the back of the booth and the wall. It would be found eventually but with luck not before morning when the cleaning staff came on duty. He inspected himself. The gray trousers were not out of the ordinary. Nor was his white Sunday shirt. But that long-tailed bow tie in school colors . . . he pulled it off and thrust it in with the blazer. He felt better, more anonymous.

Rather than ask questions of the officials, he wandered around the terminus discovering things. There was a wall map of stations served, and he looked for Reading. He had already decided this offered his best chance of getting into the County—the border was only a few miles north of there. There was a fare list underneath and he had a shock when he saw the price of a ticket. It was £11.5, two pounds more than he had in his wallet. But those were adult fares; his own would only be half. He would have very little left all the same.

A train was due to leave in twenty minutes. Rob put

money in the machine and dialed a ticket. It was a long time since breakfast, which had been no better than usual, and he was hungry. The buffet was showing on its HV advertiser a succession of the meals available inside. A chicken turned on a spit, golden brown and ten times larger than life, and was split to be dropped on a huge plate with a vast heap of crisp French fried potatoes. The set was fitted with smell, which drifted out in an agonizing assault on his nostrils. On the moving band overhead the sign winked:

THIS DISH . . . TODAY . . . ONLY £2.25 . . .

Rob swallowed and turned away. He found a Servomat and for fifty pence got a sandwich and a biscuit. The sandwich was made with wafer-thin ham and he still felt hungry when he had finished. He headed for the train. It was fifteen minutes before it was due to leave but he needed to get away from the smell of the advertising box. To his surprise both cars were almost full. He could not imagine why so many people would be wanting to go to Reading on a Sunday afternoon until he heard people in front of him talking about the Carnival.

Carnivals were held in different parts of the Conurbs at different times. They involved a lot of eating and drinking, parades, dancing in the streets—a general confusion of merry-making to which people flocked from miles, even scores of miles, around. His plan had been to take a bus to a point as far north of the town as he could, then to make his way on foot toward the border. But carnivals disrupted everything. Buses would be running erratically or not at all.

He had time to get off. He could aim for somewhere else within reach of the border—Chelmsford, say. But he did not have enough money for a second ticket and he could only change this one by going to the Information Office and asking one of the officials, who in turn might ask awkward questions. It was better to sit tight.

The piped music in the car broke off for a moment replaced by a four-note carillon heralding departure. As it swelled up again the train slid out from the terminus along its gleaming band of steel.

The journey took less than twenty minutes, the train at its fastest traveling at more than a hundred and twenty-five miles an hour. The ride was very smooth with only a slight rocking on the curves. Beneath the pillars supporting the rail there were glimpses of the city's streets. On either side high-rise blocks stretched away. Then came the stretches of Green Belt, studded with artificial lakes, fair grounds, amusement centers—everything the Conurbans needed for pleasure and distraction. Even at this high speed one saw the crowds.

There were crowds in Reading, too, filling the square outside the station. Loudspeakers broadcast music and announcements. When Rob came out they were playing a popular song, "You Are Mine, I Am Yours," and everyone was singing it in unison. There were no buses to be seen, no vehicles of any kind.

The music stopped and a giant voice, echoing since it came from several directions simultaneously, said, "Are we all happy?"

"Yes!" from a full-throated chorus.

"Then stay with Uncle, folks and folkesses. In a few minutes, a very few minutes, the Bubble Girls will dance for your delight, floating above your heads on their transparent bubbles. Seven lovely ladies who never make a wrong step. Give them a cheer to show you want to see them!"

The crowd cheered. Rob approached a cheerful red-faced man, about forty. "Excuse me. Can you tell me where I can get a bus?"

"A bus? What do you want a bus for?" He was a bit drunk, Rob realized. "You want to stay and see the show. They're good. I've seen them."

"I'm afraid I can't."

"Of course you can. It's Carnival."

Rob shook his head. The eyes in the red face narrowed in suspicion.

"What are you here for, anyway? You're not local, or you'd know the bus routes."

"I've come to see an aunt of mine. She's sick."

"On your own?"

"My mother's already here, staying with her." He tried feverishly to think of things that would make the story seem convincing. "My father couldn't get away. He works on Sundays."

"So you're on your own."

The tone was different, sympathetic now. The man called above the music. "Hey! There's a boy here needs to get to his aunt who's sick. He's come a long way on his own. Anyone got a car parked near to give him a lift?"

Rob protested. "No, it's all right. I can get there on the bus. I just wanted . . ."

Volunteers were already appearing. Good will was one

of the vaunted features of Carnival, along with the drinking and feasting and having fun. Of the early stages of Carnival, at any rate. Rob's protests were generously overridden. The red man accepted an offer on his behalf from someone who said he had a car parked only a few minutes' walk away.

Rob made a last try: "But the Bubble Dancers . . ."

"See them anytime," the volunteer said briskly. He was in his twenties, wearing a badge with interlinked rings that showed he was a professional sportsman. "Let's get you to that sick aunt. Where does she live?"

Rob thought quickly again. "It's Sheffield Road. Number 131."

The sportsman's bow furrowed. "Where's that?"

"Reading North." That was the area he wanted. "But I don't need . . ."

Someone else said: "We can ask up there."

"Sure," the sportsman agreed. "We'll find it. Come and join in the hunt for Sheffield Road, mates. My car's a ten-seater."

Doing odd things was another Carnival tradition. The sportsman was obviously pleased about his ten-seater—there was only one electrocar model larger. He collected a group of eight, including the red-faced man, and they set off. Rob went with them unprotestingly. He would have to hope for an opportunity to slip away later; it was impossible here.

Electrocars, like the buses, were fitted with governors that controlled the power input from the cables and so, theoretically, the speed. There was additionally a separate and lower limit for inner-city streets. The sportsman not only disregarded that but clearly had managed to disconnect the governor. They tore through the streets with the other men cheering him on. Fortunately there was almost no traffic and no sign of police, who would be busy controlling the Carnival.

Progress was slower when they reached North End. They stopped the car at intervals to ask for Sheffield Road. (What if there was a Sheffield Road, Rob wondered, and a number 131?) He was hoping for a chance to break away but none came. One person directed them to a place which proved to be Shafford Road. They were getting tired of the search and a bit irritable.

One of them said: "Over there. Police station."

"Not to worry," the sportsman said. "Not breaking any limits, not at the minute."

"We could ask them. They're bound to know."

They immediately brightened up. It was a square steel and concrete building, ugly but massive. The sportsman stopped the car and he and most of the others piled out.

It would take them less than a minute to find that Sheffield Road did not exist. Then the police would either come out to the car, or he would be taken in. One of the men was still beside him, placidly smoking a cheroot.

"I feel a bit dizzy, . . ." Rob said, "some fresh air."

The smoker puffed and nodded. The last of the group was disappearing into the police station as Rob got out. The road was long and straight but thirty yards away there was an intersection. He ran for it full pelt.

There were shouts behind him. Glancing back as he reached the intersection he saw them coming after him. The sportsman was in the lead, pounding along with frightening speed and determination. This road was made up of mono-lithic modern blocks with lawn surrounds dotted with small bushes. No cover at all. If the side road offered no more . . .

He was in luck though. It was a street of small, rotting, last-century houses, stuck together in pairs, all red brick and pebble-dash. He ran down an alley to the right which gave onto another lying between the backs of the houses in this street and those in one parallel to it. No cover again, just a rough track puddled from the previous day's rain. But there were narrow strips of garden between the alley and the houses, many of them with sheds at the end. Rob could hear his pursuers halloing behind him. He dodged through a wire fence, pulled open the door of a shed, and crouched inside.

There was no window. It was pitch-dark and had an odd pungent smell. He heard the pursuit tear noisily past. The trouble was that, having lost him, they were likely to back-track and search more thoroughly. After a time in fact he heard them returning. Then he was startled by a voice just the other side of the thin wooden wall.

"Looking for someone?"

"A boy, about thirteen." It sounded like the sportsman. "Seen anything of him?"

It must be the owner of the shed and he must have seen Rob go in and come down from the house to investigate. Now he would open the door and hand him over.

"White shirt, gray trousers?" the man asked.

"That's him! He's brought us out here on a wild-goose chase. We'll give him carnival pranks when we lay hands on him. It will be a long time before he pulls another one."

"Yes, I saw him. He dodged up through the Millers' garden. That's two houses along."

"Then we've got him!"

"I wouldn't be sure about that. He could have got through the side to the front and off along Kirkup Road."

"Thanks! Come on, then. We're wasting time."

They thudded off. Rob lay waiting. He wondered why the man had protected him. If they were to find they had been tricked he would be in bad trouble himself. People swung between extremes during Carnival and violence was common. They were quite capable of wrecking his house.

Rob had been aware of small scuffling noises. When the door opened, bringing a shaft of light, he realized the significance of the acrid smell. On a bench against one wall were several small boxes with wire netting across the front. There were small furry animals in them. Rabbits.

"You can get along. They've gone," the man said.

He was thin and sharp featured, with dirty shirt sleeves rolled up under a tattered sleeveless pullover and trousers patched at the knee. He did not look like someone given to risky or generous acts. The explanation, Rob saw, lay in the rabbits, kept here in this windowless almost airless shed. It was prohibited to keep livestock without a license, and he would never get one. He probably fattened them to sell to a butcher. There was a market for nonfactory meat.

"On your way," the man said.

There was nothing Rob would have liked more. The smell was getting unpleasant. On the other hand . . .

"They're probably still nearby," he said. "And the police may be looking. If they catch me . . ."

He saw it register in the narrow wary face. Rob might tell them where he had hidden. The man nodded.

"Right."

He closed the door as Rob was saying: "Half an hour would probably do." A key turned in the lock. It must have been an accident that it was not locked earlier; perhaps he had just gone up to the house to get something. Rob settled down, his back against the wall, trying to ignore the smell. It was better than being beaten up by his hunters or handed to the police to be taken back to school. He wrinkled his nose. Half an hour was bearable.

He had no watch. Juniors at the boarding school were not allowed them. It was difficult to assess the passage of time, especially in the dark. He tried counting seconds and minutes to himself but had to give up. It made things drag still more.

Eventually he realized that well over half an hour had passed, over an hour probably. He tried the door to see if he could shake it open but the shed was more firmly built than it seemed. He sat down again. The smell of the rabbits did not improve and he did not get used to it. He got a cramp and had to get up to ease his aching muscles.

Time passed very slowly. Could the man have abandoned him? But he would have to see to the rabbits. Or could he have met with an accident? He had looked like someone living on his own; it might be days before anyone investigated. Of course, he could probably attract attention by shouting —someone would hear him eventually. But whoever did would very likely turn him over to the police. He was wondering how long he could stick it when he heard footsteps and, a moment later, the door opened.

Very little light came in. The sky behind the man's head was gray with dusk—it must be around eight in the evening. Rob came out stiffly. Fresh air made him feel faint.

"Nothing to stop you going now," the man said.

There was something else besides faintness. Free of the stink of rabbits he was ravenously hungry. Apart from the sandwich and biscuit he had eaten nothing since early morning. The bar of chocolate was in his case and the case had been left in the car when he made a dash for it.

"I'm hungry," he said. "Could you give me something?"

The man looked as though he might refuse, then nodded. "Wait here."

He went up to the house and came back with a paper bag. "Take it away and eat it." His tone was grudging.

Rob could see he was anxious to get him away. "The County's not far from here, is it?" he asked.

"Not far."

"What's the best way?"

"What do you want to go there for?"

The tone this time was not grudging but amazed.

"I just want to."

"You must be mad," the man said. "And anyway there's the Barrier. Wire fences fifty, a hundred feet high, with electricity running through. Char you to a cinder if you put a finger to them."

"What about gates?"

"None. Patrols, though. With dogs that kill you on sight."

They were the sort of rumors Rob had heard before, but more frightening when he had the prospect of testing the truth of them.

"You won't get within a mile of it," the man said.

"I'll get far enough to forget I was ever here. Are you going to feed the rabbits tonight?"

The man's face tightened and Rob thought for a moment he would hit him. But he said, "It's your own lookout." He pointed down the alley. "That takes you into Chepstow Street. Turn left and you're heading north. Keep on that way and you'll reach nomansland in a mile or two. After that . . ." He shrugged. "I've no idea how far it is."

"Thanks," Rob said. "And for the food."

He set off along the alley. The man watched him go, a silent fading figure in the twilight.

This was plainly a poor part of the town and it got worse. The streets were meaner, the houses more and more dilapidated. You could see in the light of the street lamps that they needed repairs, a coat of paint. The street lamps themselves were of the old-fashioned electric-bulb kind. They had probably been there for a hundred years and looked even older.

It was dark by now, though there was a half-moon fitfully appearing between scudding banks of cloud. A breeze had got up and Rob found himself shivering. He could have done with a jersey but that too had been lost with the case. He was cold and hungry. He thought of the food he had got from the man with the rabbits but decided it might attract attention to eat it as he walked.

When he came out of the alley he had checked that north roughly coincided with the position of the moon, low in the sky, and had continued in this direction through the warren of roads and houses. He had reached a part where there were not even the little two-seater electrocars because no cables had been laid. There were few people about— more and more of the houses he passed were empty. Then he came to a crossroads and saw that the continuation of the road was unlit. Not only were the lamps out, but the houses on either side stood dark and deserted. In the moonlight he could see that the road extended for perhaps fifty yards, and that beyond was open ground.

People, he knew, did not like living over by nomansland. That was why the houses had not been pulled down but left to rot: if they were demolished there would be a new edge and people would move away from that in turn. Rob found himself shivering, not just with cold but at the sight of darkness, the thought of the emptiness beyond. All his life, like everyone else in the Conurbs, he had been surrounded by the comforting presence of others—all the millions of them. Being glad to have a little privacy occasionally was not the same as wanting to go out there, alone.

He wondered whether he ought not to lie up until morning. In that house on the corner, say, from which one could see the street lamp under which he now stood. The door was probably not locked, and anyway one could get in through the glassless windows. It might be better to cross nomansland by day when one could see the way. There was the electrified fence to think of, and the possibility of stumbling into it in the dark.

But traveling by day meant more chance of being seen as well as seeing. The moon, which had gone behind cloud, sailed out into a sea of stars and taking the sign for encouragement he walked on.

4

A Rider in the Sun

Grass grew in the crumbling street and the front gardens of the houses were choked with bushes. In one place a quite large sapling grew out through an empty window frame. Where the road ended there was open country, dotted with trees and undergrowth. A noise somewhere ahead, sepulchral hooting, startled him. He realized it must be an owl, but he had never heard one before except in holovision thrillers. He had seen them, of course, in the zoo, but silent, sitting hunched and blinking.

Rob fought an impulse to turn back, and plodded northward. There was a fair light from the moon but the ground was uneven. He put his foot in a hole and almost fell. The coldness and hunger were worse and the thought of a warm bed, even one likely to be surrounded by tormentors at any moment, was an attractive one. He decided he could at least do something about the hunger, and opened up the paper bag. There was bread and cheese. In the moonlight he could see that the cheese had mildew on it and the bread was stale and hard, a week old at least. He might have known the man with the rabbits would not have given him food he could eat himself. Still he was hungry enough to eat anything. He crunched the bread with his teeth and bit alternately at the hunk of cheese. It was sour but it filled his stomach. He felt thirsty now, but there was nothing to be done about that.

He went on, his back to the glow of light which was the Conurb, into a night lit only by the half-moon and a scatter of stars. He could not have imagined such loneliness. The urge to give up, to turn back toward the comfort and warmth of his fellow men, was almost overpowering. Once he did stop and look around. The glow stretched in a band across the southern horizon, made up of millions of lumo-globes, neon signs, electrocar headlights, display illuminations. It would diminish as the night wore on, but it would never completely die. There was always light in the Conurbs. Resolutely he turned again and walked away from it.

The ground was rising and dimly in the distance he could see the slopes of the hills. When he had been traveling for two or three hours the moon went behind a cloud. But the sky was mostly clear. He saw the stars, sharp and bright against deep black. The glow of the Conurb had become a faraway smudge. He had never seen such a sky before because of the other lights all around. It was breath-taking to see how many stars there were, to look at the diamond dust of the Milky Way. Breath-taking, and frightening. He shivered and resumed his march. The moon came out, a small comfort.

There were sounds, mostly unidentifiable, more or less alarming. A howling which could have been one of the wild dogs which were supposed to run in packs in nomansland, fortunately a long way off. Squeaks and rustlings and clickings. Once, almost under his feet, a hoarse grunting which made him jump away. Later he was to learn that it was nothing more terrible than a hedgehog, but at the time it was horrifying.

Rob wondered, as he had done a score of times already, how far he was from the Barrier; and in that instant saw it. Moonlight gleamed on metal farther up the slope. He advanced cautiously and investigated. Nothing like a hundred feet high, or even fifty. About twelve. It was constructed of diamond wire mesh, supported by heavy metal posts a dozen or so feet apart. That was as much as could be made out. The obviously sensible course, now he had found it, was to wait until daylight and examine it then.

He found a hollow in the ground, somewhat protected from the wind, and lay down and tried to sleep. It was not easy. He felt the cold more keenly, having stopped walking, and the bread and cheese lay heavily on his stomach. In the end he had to get up and walk about, slapping his arms to restore circulation. He alternated lying and exercising while the hours of night crawled past. Eventually, worn out, he fell asleep and shivered through dreams for an hour. When he awoke from one in which the Master of Discipline was accusing him of having a nonaligned eye and several limbs out of place, to the accompaniment of jeers and howls from the prefects, there was a different, wider and paler light all around. Dawn was breaking.

Rob slapped himself into something like life—he was tired and cold, hungry again, and aching from sleeping on ground, which made the hard mattresses of the boarding school seem like plastifoam. He went to the fence and looked at it. It ran as far as he could see in either direction, straight to the east, curving inward and out of sight to the west. The mesh was in a pattern of half-inch diamonds, the metal supports several inches thick and sunk in concrete blocks. The bottom of the fence disappeared into the ground. Electrified? He did not feel like touching it to try.

He looked through the mesh. It seemed no different there —open grassland and trees in the distance. The ground rising to a near horizon. Farther off, featureless hills. He decided he might as well walk on, to the west since it looked less depressing than the long line of fence to the east.

He came to a part where there were more trees on this side, some growing quite close to the fence. If there were one right up against it which he could climb . . . Or if, for that matter, he had one of the long flexipoles used by jumpers in the Games, and the skill to vault with it, he could get over very easily. But there wasn't, and he hadn't. He checked, glimpsing something, a small flash of movement, on a branch of a tree ahead of him. A small brown shape. Something else known only from the zoo: a squirrel.

It stayed on the branch for several seconds, sitting up with its paws to its face, nibbling something or washing itself. Then it whisked back toward the trunk and down to the ground. Rob lost sight of it when it disappeared into grass. Not long after, though, he saw it again, this time racing up and over the fence! That solved one problem. He put a finger, tentative still, against the mesh. It was cold, harmless metal.

He still had to find a way of getting over it. He was no squirrel. The small-gauge and the smooth poles offered no kind of toehold. There was nothing for it but to carry on walking. At least it helped him forget how cold it was. The sky behind him was pale blue, beginning to flush gold with the invisible sun. But it was cold enough. There were places where the grass crackled with frost.

He found the answer at last in a minor landslip. The hill had crumbled slightly, above and below the fence, and rain had washed the loose soil down. It did not amount to much but the steel mesh instead of running down into the ground showed a gap underneath. It was no more than an inch or so, but it gave him the idea. He squatted down and set to work enlarging it. The ground was friable but it was not easy. His fingertips burned with cold. He kept at it. Bit by bit he dug earth away until there was a gap he thought he could wriggle through. But he had been too optimistic and had to go back to digging.

The second time he made it. He scratched himself on the sharp base of the mesh and had a moment's panic when he stuck half way, but he managed at last. He stood up shakily. He was in the County.

The slope still shortened his horizon to the north, but the brow was no more than fifty yards away. It should offer a

vantage point. Rob climbed it, and climbed into the
warmth and brightness of the rising sun. A bird was singing
far up in the sky; he looked for it but could not find it. All
was blueness and emptiness.

He stood at the top of the rise and looked around. There
were hills on either side, the sun's orb just clear of one to
the east. He was dazzled by sunlight and had difficulty taking in the landscape before him. It went down in a gentle
fall and was not wild but patterned with fields and hedges.
To the left a cart track led in the distance to a lane. To the
right . . . He dropped to the ground. A man was staring
toward him.

He thought he must have been seen: the man was no
more than thirty yards away and he must have been out-
lined against the sky. But the man did not move as seconds
passed. Rob's eyes, growing accustomed to the bright sunlight, took in details. A face that was not a face. Where legs
should have emerged from old-fashioned black trousers
there were sticks. A scarecrow, in fact. He had read of them
in an old book.

It stood in the center of a ploughed field. He went across
and looked at it. Turnip face with eyes and mouth roughly
cut, a worn black suit stuffed with straw. The trousers were
badly holed, the jacket torn under the sleeve but otherwise
in fair condition. Rob fingered the cloth and then undid the
front buttons and pulled it off. Straw fell around his feet.
He shook dust and insects from it. When he put it on it felt
cold and damp but he reckoned it would soon warm up. It
would make a difference the coming night if he were still
sleeping out. It was too big, of course. He turned the sleeves

back inside which improved things, though it bagged around his chest. The scarecrow looked sadly naked—solid to the waist but above just a turnip head supported on a stick. Rob looked closely at the head. A bit mildewed but it might be edible. He decided he was not quite hungry enough for that.

He went roughly northwest. There were different crops in the fields. In one big field there were rows of small green-leaved plants with tiny purple flowers. Would they bear some kind of fruit in due course? They would have to be very small. He pulled at one and it came up with white oval things hanging from its roots. Potatoes, he recognized. He could not cook them, but filled the pockets of his jacket in case he found a means later.

His feet were tired and aching from the unaccustomed walking but he pressed on, leaving the fence as far behind him as possible. He rested from time to time, and once while doing so heard a new sound. It grew louder and clarified into something which he had at least heard on holo-vision historical epics—the thudding of horses' hooves.

Rob took cover behind a nearby hedge. It had a view of the lane and soon the horsemen appeared, riding to the west. There were half a dozen, in red tunics with gold buttons and gleaming leather straps and belts. They rode with careless arrogance; he heard them calling to one another and laughing. A couple of big dogs, one yellow, one white with black spots, lolloped alongside, their mouths open, red tongues hanging from between white teeth. And the horsemen had swords: the scabbards rattled against their high brown leather boots.

They did not look his way. The cavalcade rode on, disappearing behind high hedges, the sound of their passing gradually fading on the morning air. The king's musketeers must have looked something like that, riding through the summer fields near Paris on their way to a brush with the cardinal's men. It was more storybook than real; fascinating but scarcely believable.

Not long afterward he saw the first house inside the County. It had outlying buildings, a small pond, and poultry pecked the ground nearby. A farmhouse. There would be food there, but he dared not approach. Smoke rose from a chimney and as he watched a figure came from one of the outbuildings, crossed the yard, and disappeared inside the house. Going to breakfast, perhaps. Rob felt in his pocket and brought out one of the tiny potatoes. Friction had rubbed it clean of earth. He bit into it. It tasted unpleasant insofar as it tasted of anything, but he managed to chew it and get it down. It quenched his thirst a little, too. He ate three or four more.

The day wore on. During one of his rests he took off the jacket and rolled it up as a pillow for his head. He fell asleep and woke with the sun burning his face. It was high in the sky, almost at the zenith. He chewed more potatoes and went limping on his way. His feet were hurting him. A mile or so farther on he stopped at the edge of a field and took off his socks. His feet were blistered and some of the blisters had burst, exposing raw flesh.

He realized he could not go on indefinitely like this, but did not know what else to do. Field had succeeded field, with little change. There were animals in some which he knew were cows. One obtained milk from cows, but how? And anyway the sight of them made him nervous. In other fields there were men and machines. He could not tell precisely what the machines were doing because he had given them as wide a berth as possible. They were silent, presumably powered by fuel cells. He had also kept clear of houses, not that there were many. The emptiness of this land, which had been surprising and troubling, was becoming monotonous, mind wearying. Rob looked at his swollen feet. He wondered if it would be better to lie up in the shade. But would he be any better able to go on later in the day?

And what was he hoping to achieve? He had come here spurred by hatred of the school, and by the discovery that his mother had been born and lived her early life in the County. He had had this idea of farmlands as places that produced food, but it was not turning out like that. All he had found—all it seemed he would find—were a few small raw potatoes.

He might as well, he thought miserably, give himself up. He would have to do that eventually, or starve.

Someone called in the distance and he looked up quickly. There was a man on horseback in the gap at the end of the field. The call had been to Rob from him. There was a way through to another field on the left, and a wood not far off. If he could only reach it . . . The horseman had started to come forward. He decided he had no time to put on socks and shoes. He grabbed them and ran.

The field into which he emerged was long but narrow—it was only twenty yards or so to a high hedge separating it

from the next field which in turn was bordered by the
wood. There was no gap, but Rob 'saw a place where it
looked thin enough for him to squeeze through. He made
it with thorns tearing at him and thought he was safe: the
horseman would have to find a longer way around and by
the time he did Rob would be in the wood. He could surely
dodge a man on horseback there. His feet were hurting
horribly but he disregarded that. Thirty yards to the wood,
perhaps less. He heard another call and glanced over his
shoulder. Horse and rider were in midair, clearing the hedge
in a jump.

He tried to squeeze extra strength out of his legs. Twenty
yards, ten, and hooves thudding in his wake. He would not
reach the sanctuary. He wondered if the horseman would
ride him down, or slash him with his sword. Then his left
foot turned under him and he crashed to the ground. The
impact dazed and winded him. He lay gasping and heard
the sound of hooves slacken and cease. The horse was snort-
ing quite close and above him.

Rob looked up. The sun was behind the rider's right
shoulder and he could not see him properly for the glare.
There was an impression of fairness, of a blue shirt open at
the neck. He looked for the sword but could not see one.

The horse moved, jigging, and the rider checked it. The
light fell at a different angle and now Rob could see him
clearly. He was not a man but a fair-haired boy, not much
older than himself.

5

The Cave

In a quick easy movement the rider vaulted from the saddle. Holding the reins with one hand he extended the other to Rob.

"Are you all right?" he asked. "Let me help you up."

He spoke in a kind of drawl, very confident and assured. Rob got to his feet, wincing. The boy let go of the reins and put both hands reassuringly to Rob's arms.

"You're barefooted," he said with surprise. "Your feet are bleeding. Here, you'd better sit down and we'll have a look at them."

Rob was still clutching one shoe—the other, and his socks, he had dropped in the last part of his flight. He did as he was told and the fair-haired boy squatted beside him. His hair was almost gold in color, thick and gleaming on top but cropped close at the back and sides. It fell forward as he lifted Rob's feet and examined them.

"Not too good. Hang on, I've got some water." He went to the horse and removed a flat, leather-covered flask from the saddle. He poured water into one hand and gently bathed the feet. "They really need dressing."

"Is there any water left? I'm a bit thirsty," Rob said.

"Help yourself."

Rob drank and handed the flask back.

"You're not a countryman, are you?" the boy said.

"Countryman," he discovered later, was a term used both for farm workers and servants of the gentry.

"I'm from the Conurb."

The fair boy stared at him. "How did you get here?"

"Across the fence. Well, under it really."

There was no point in trying to conceal things. He could not get away. The pain in his feet, which he had disregarded while running, was much worse. He wondered whether the boy would make him walk to the nearest police station. And then? He supposed they would take him back to the school but did not much care. He was more angry with himself for having failed, and failed so soon.

There had been a pause. The boy broke it. "I'm Mike Gifford. What's your name?"

Rob told him.

"I've never met anyone from the Conurb. What's it like there?"

Rob gave a gesture of helplessness. "It's a bit difficult to say, just like that."

"I suppose it would be. What made you come here, anyway?"

He made an attempt to answer that, explaining roughly what had happened since his father's death and what he had learned about his mother. He spoke of his experiences at the school.

"Tough," Mike said. "They give you a rough time at the start at my place, but not as bad as that." He stared at Rob. "The question is: what now?"

He had been decent so far. It might be worth appealing to him.

"You could just forget about finding me."

"And then?"

"I'll manage."

"You're crippled. You won't be able to walk for days on those feet."

"I can lie up somewhere."

Mike shook his head. "Not a chance."

The tone was casual but decisive. It had been too much to hope, Rob thought. He remained silent. After a moment or two, Mike said, "How would you live? Do you know how to trap a rabbit, for instance—skin and cook it?"

"No."

"I could manage better." It was not a boast but a statement of fact. "I mean, I could kill game and cook it—that sort of thing. But I wouldn't like to have to live that way for long."

"I thought I might get work of some kind. I don't mind what."

"Bit young, aren't you? And they'd want to know where you came from. Countrymen don't usually move far from their own village."

He spoke judiciously but it was plain that he thought it a completely harebrained scheme. As it was, Rob realized.

"You're going to report me?"

"We need time to think," Mike said. "If I could hide you somewhere for the present . . . It's lucky that I'm at home. I ought to have been back at school but I was ill last term and I'm still convalescent. I had glandular fever and then a go of brain fever afterward. So I'm supposed to be taking things easy."

He did not look ill; the reverse in fact.

"I could make myself some sort of a shelter in the wood, perhaps."

"No good," Mike said, frowning. "The keepers are pretty thorough. I could smuggle you into the house, but it wouldn't be safe. My parents and Cecily might not spot you but the servants would. It will have to be outside. Not the stables, because of the grooms." He snapped his fingers. "I think I've got it. A cave I found farther up the valley. Well, not so much a cave as a kind of building underground. We could fit it up for you, and I could bring food."

Could it work? It would give him a chance to lie up, to recuperate. He felt grateful but in a distant, almost disbelieving way. He did not know why the fair-haired boy wanted to help him. A trap of some kind? But at least it was a reprieve.

"I don't mind what it's like," he said.

"The men will be up in the top fields this afternoon so I could take you around by the river. I'll put you up on Captain."

Captain was presumably the horse.

"I think I can manage to walk."

"No." The refusal had authority. "I'll go and pick up the stuff you dropped. Better get your shoes and socks on for now and we'll see about dressing your feet later."

Rob did so, wincing. Mike showed him how to mount the horse, explaining how you had to twist the stirrup and stand facing the horse's tail. He spoke soothingly to the horse as Rob scrambled on.

He seemed to be a long way from the ground. And the animal underneath him was unstable, shifting its feet and pulling against Mike's hands holding the reins. Mike called out, "Whoah! Steady, boy. Take it easy."

The horse quietened but Rob still felt unhappy about it.

"Take the reins," Mike ordered. "I'll hang on to the snaffle."

They moved and Rob felt the jolt of the hooves under him. If it was as uncomfortable as this just walking, he wondered, what must galloping be like?

The river ran through a small valley, much closer to one side than the other. A road followed the near bank and above that was wooded country. They had come close to the road at one point and Rob saw that it was brown in color; like earth, but too smooth to be earth. He asked about it, and Mike explained.

"It's a plastic. You have different surfaces in the Conurb?

I suppose you would. This is specially made for horses. It's fairly soft and resilient—easy on the hooves."

"Doesn't it wear quickly?"

Mike shrugged. "Depends how much use it gets. It's only used for horses and carriages, of course. And it's fairly easily repaired. There's a machine that lays and smooths it at about a mile an hour. Look, I'm afraid you're going to have to foot it the rest of the way. I can't get Captain any farther through the trees. It's not far now, though."

"That's all right. How do I get off?"

"Just cock your leg over." He watched critically as Rob struggled to dismount. "Hang on while I tie him up."

The horse whinnied after him as they went away.

"Want to hold on to me?"

"No, thanks." Rob gritted his teeth. "I'm all right."

In places they had to force a way through undergrowth. Mike commented that it was a good thing; it was less likely that anyone else would come this way. They were on rising ground, thick with trees of different kinds and sizes. After ten minutes they broke through into a more open space looking up to the crest of the hill, a grassy hump overgrown with brambles and creepers. Rob looked for the cave but could see nothing.

"Bearing up?" Mike asked. "Over here."

He led the way across the clearing to a point where the brambles ended. Carefully he pulled at a tangle of thorn. It came clear and there was a way behind it. You had to squeeze close to the side of the hill on one side; on the other you were concealed by the undergrowth.

Mike, pushing ahead of him, said, "I found it when Tess

went in after a rabbit. That's my dog. I thought I might turn it into a den or something, but I never did. I left it covered so that no one else would find it. Here we are."

There was an opening, framed in crumbling concrete, about three feet wide and four high. Rob ducked to follow Mike in. It was dark, because very little light filtered through the tangle of leaves and briars outside. Rob could just see that they were in some sort of chamber, a six-foot cube or thereabouts. Like the doorway it was built of concrete.

"What was it for?" he asked. "Who would want to build something like this, inside a hill?"

"There's more of it higher up but it's broken and overgrown. I think this was just an extra way out. It was probably a gun battery—for firing at aircraft. Something out of the Hitler War, anyway."

"As old as that?"

"Maybe older. They had aircraft in the previous war, too, didn't they?" He looked around. "It's a bit rough. Do you think you'll be all right?"

"I'll be all right."

"We can make some improvements. I'll go and get a few things now. You don't have to stay in here as long as you dodge back if you hear anyone coming up through the wood. When I come back, I'll whistle." He demonstrated a call on two notes. "O.K.?"

Rob nodded. "O.K."

He waited lying out in the grass. Trees and the hill cut off most of the sky but there was a patch of sunlight. The silence and isolation, the dark alien quality of the wood, troubled him a little. Mike was a long time gone. The patch of sunlight moved away from the clearing and now lit only the side of the hill above the brambles. It was less warm and he shivered. He dismissed a suspicion that Mike might have had second thoughts: there was something about him which was dependable. Two rabbits appeared from the wood and he watched them, fascinated. It was hard to believe he was really here, in the County, with plants budding, wild things living all around him. And yet already this was the reality, the Conurb—with its packed streets, high-rise buildings, crawling electrocars—the fantasy.

The rabbits pricked up their ears and in a moment, with a flash of white tail, were gone. He heard Mike's whistle below in the wood.

He was heavily weighted down, a large bundle slung over one shoulder and a bag in his right hand. He dropped them on the grass and said, "Sorry I've taken so long. It seemed a good idea to tackle things as thoroughly as possible." He kicked the bundle. "Blankets and a pillow. I think I can get a camp bed up eventually but for the present it will have to be a hard lie. You won't freeze to death, though. No sheets, I'm afraid."

"Thanks."

"How are those feet?"

"Not too bad."

"Let's have a go at them."

He watched while Rob gingerly removed shoes and socks. The rubbed blisters had been bleeding again.

"One snag is that the nearest water is ten minutes away," Mike said. "They could really do with bathing properly.

But I've got some antiseptic tissues which will clean them up. May smart a bit."

It did. Rob found himself involuntarily drawing his foot away as Mike dabbed at the raw patches. Mike did not apologize but gripped the foot more securely and carried on. When he had finished the cleaning he applied adhesive dressings. He took a rolled pair of socks out of the bag and tossed them to Rob.

"Put those on." He looked at the discarded pair which were worn into holes. "No point in keeping these. I'll ditch them somewhere. Are you feeling hungry?"

"I had some stale bread and moldy cheese last night, and a few raw potatoes today. Yes, I'm hungry."

"Well, you're going to have bread and cheese again. It was all I could lay hands on. But at least it's not stale or moldy."

He produced a loaf and a hunk of cheese, wrapped in a muslin cloth.

"Have you got a knife?" Rob shook his head. "You didn't come as well prepared as you might have done for an expedition like this, did you?"

The comment, though amiable in tone, was a bit scathing.

"I didn't have a lot of time to prepare anything," Rob replied. "And I ran away from school on Sunday, when the shops were closed."

"Don't you carry a pocket knife?"

"In the Conurb? Not unless you want trouble with the police. They're called offensive weapons."

Mike shook his head, uncomprehendingly. "Better have

this." He unclipped a heavy bone-handled knife from his belt. "Keep it. I've got another at home. I'll nip along and get some water while you're eating. I've brought a jerry can."

He took it and went off through the wood. Rob started hungrily on the food. The bread was brown and crusty, soft and white inside. Both smell and taste were new, and far better than anything he was used to. The same was true of the cheese which was golden yellow, smooth and strong. Rob ate half, and half the loaf, and wrapped up the remainder. He heard Mike's whistle and saw him appear carrying the jerry can full of water. He drank thirstily.

"I'll get cups and stuff in due course," Mike said. "Let's get the gear inside and out of the way."

In the near darkness of the concrete cell they put things down. While Rob was unpacking blankets, Mike fiddled with something like a portable lumoglobe but with a different, less regular shape. He brought out a pocket lighter and lit it with a naked flame. A soft light bloomed. Rob asked him what it was.

"This? Oil lamp. No, I don't suppose you would have them on your side. I'll have to bring oil up, but it's full at the moment. You'd better have this lighter, too." It was not very different in principle to those sold in the Conurb, but heavy and silvery in color instead of being light and brightly patterned. "Look, it will be better if you use the inner room as your base."

A low doorway at the back led to another slightly larger cell. In the corner were steps leading upward. Mike held the lamp forward.

"That's the way up to the main part I told you about. It's blocked with rubble. Stay here. I'm just going outside to see if the light shows." Returning, he said: "I'm fairly sure it's O.K., but you'd probably better recheck after dark. If it does get through you can probably rig up one of the blankets as a screen."

Rob nodded.

"I'm going to leave you now," Mike said. "I have a tutor who comes around since I'm not at school. I'm late for him already. You'll be all right?"

"Yes. Thanks for everything."

Mike made a dismissive gesture. "I'll get along as early as I can tomorrow. You don't have to stick in here, but be careful when you're outside. Make sure you don't leave traces." He grinned. "Sleep well."

Time passed very slowly. Rob did go outside but no farther than the clearing. He had moments of elation at having found a refuge, alternating with depression in which he thought he might as well have turned back or given himself up for the good it would do him in the long run. And loneliness. It was bad enough in the clearing, much worse inside the four blank walls of the cell, watching his shadow on the wall.

Dusk came and deepened into night. He checked outside for light showing; then went in and ate the remainder of the bread and cheese. He decided after that he might as well go to bed. He rolled himself into the blankets and put out the lamp.

He was very tired, having had so little sleep the night before, and expected to drop off quickly. The hardness of the floor proved no bar to this, but he thought again of his isolation, inside a hill, surrounded by dark rustling trees. And animals? He came awake on that. There was nothing frightening about rabbits, but what of others? Were there bigger ones roaming loose—wolves maybe? He thought he heard something and strained his ears uselessly to catch and identify the sound.

Sleep had gone. He put on the lamp again and peered into the outer room. Nothing. He rigged up a barrier in the doorway, with the bag and the jerry can. It would not even keep a rabbit out but it might give him a slight warning of anything trying to get in.

He was awake for a long time and then slept heavily. He awoke to a hand on his shoulder and looked up blinking to see Mike standing over him.

"Sorry to disturb you. I've brought some sausages and I thought you'd like to eat them while they're fairly hot. Coffee, too. How did you sleep, by the way?"

The fears of the night were only shameful fancies. "Pretty well, thanks."

Mike came up every day, sometimes more than once. He brought food and other things—soap, clean clothes, eating utensils, on the third day a collapsible wood-and-canvas bed. He asked Rob if there was anything else he would like.

"You haven't any books you could lend me, I suppose?"

"Books?" He sounded surprised.

"It gets a bit boring in the evenings," Rob said.

"Yes. I can see it would. It was just . . ." He looked at

Rob in frank inquiry. "I didn't know people read books in the Conurbs."

"Not many do."

"It's funny . . ."

"What is?"

"The way one takes things for granted," Mike said. "About the Conurbs. About the County, too, come to that. About ourselves, I suppose."

"I've thought of that, myself. About taking things for granted, I mean. Look, if it's going to be difficult . . ."

"Difficult?" Mike's expression cleared. "Not a bit. I'll bring some next time. What sort of thing do you like?"

"Historical adventures. But anything will do."

Mike brought two books, bound in rich brown leather and smelling of age. One was *Mr. Sponge's Sporting Tour*, the other *My Life on the Zambezi*. The first was about fox hunting, the second an account of life in primitive Africa in the late nineteenth or early twentieth century. Later, he asked Rob how he was getting on with them.

"All right," Rob answered cautiously.

"Surtees is good, isn't he?"

That was the author of *Mr. Sponge*.

"I don't understand much about fox hunting," Rob said. "Do you people still do it?"

"Yes, of course."

"Do you?" Mike nodded. "You like it?"

"Great stuff," Mike said. "A good run on a sharp morning—it's marvelous."

"Scores of people on horseback," Rob said, "with a pack

of hounds chasing one small animal. It's a bit unfair, isn't it?"

Mike stared at him, and in a cold voice said, "You were right in saying you don't understand it."

The critical tone reminded Rob of how much he owed Mike, and how dependent he was on him.

"You're right. There aren't any foxes in the Conurbs."

Mike looked at him for a moment, then laughed.

"No. There wouldn't be. The other book, by the way, is by some ancestor of mine. He was a missionary and eventually became a bishop. Terrible old bore, but I was in a rush and these were the first I got hold of. I'll look for some adventure stories before tomorrow."

One evening Rob ventured farther than usual. He knew roughly the way Mike took on his journey home and he followed it, staying under cover as much as possible. He came at last to the edge of a field with a view over open ground.

The road here left the river and turned sharply right, disappearing over the brow of a hill half a mile away. Almost opposite, on the far side of the road, was a large green-painted gate supported by stone pillars. From it a reddish drive ran through parkland to a house whose grounds were bounded farther down by the broad silver stripe of the river.

He knew this must be where Mike lived though it was difficult to believe that so vast a place could be the home of a single small family—Mike, his mother and father, and Cecily,

his sister. It was built of gray stone and had an irregular rambling look, as though different parts had been added at
different times. He tried to count the windows along the
front but gave up. There were more buildings at the back,
forming an L to the main structure. He saw activity there:
horses being harnessed to a carriage that was painted black
with canary yellow panels. He watched the carriage being
driven around to the front of the house. A figure which he
could see was that of a woman came down the steps from
the front door, attended by a man in blue uniform, and was
helped to enter. He heard a distant cry from the coachman
and with a toss of reins the carriage was driven away, along
the drive through the gates, to disappear where the road
climbed the hill.

He mentioned it to Mike on his next visit. Mike nodded.

"Mother, visiting the Caprons. They live five miles from
us."

"A house of that size," Rob said, "—how can you possibly
use it all? It's enormous."

"Enormous?" Mike was surprised. "Not really. Just an
average-sized manor house. As for using it all, there are the
servants, of course."

"How many?"

"Servants? I'm not quite sure. About twenty? That's the
indoor staff."

"Twenty people to look after four?"

"Something like that."

"Why do they put up with it?"

"Put up? There's nothing to put up with. They don't
have a bad life, one way and another. Not much work, and

all sorts of privileges. They reckon they're a lot better off than they would be in a Conurb: more space, better food, the country—a better life altogether. They despise the Conurbans."

"And the Conurbans despise them for living like slaves."

"Slaves!" Mike grinned. "Tell that to Gaudion, our butler. But if both lots do feel that way it's just as well, isn't it? Each satisfied with what they have and despising the others. A good arrangement all around."

There was a weird logic in it. Rob took a different tack. "Why *do* you have such primitive transport—horses and carriages instead of electrocars. They can't be as comfortable and they can't travel as fast."

"I wouldn't be too sure about the comfort. Modern carriages have a lot of little refinements, including extremely good springing. It's a very pleasant ride. And as for speed, what's the hurry? Everyone has time enough and to spare."

"I suppose so."

It did not satisfy him, though. It was one of the moments which made him realize that this was a strange and alien land—that the whole cast of Mike's mind was foreign to his.

Gradually his den took on a slightly more comfortable aspect. There were a couple of old rugs Mike had brought, a folding chair, a box which served as a table—best of all a little portable stove fueled, like the lamp, by kerosene.

He could cook things for himself, and it was often easier for Mike to bring him raw eggs, steaks and so on, than food from the larder. All the food here, he found, was different from that which he had been used to: it looked better and tasted better. He did his cooking in the outer chamber where the smells would disperse more readily into the open air. To be on the safe side he confined his activities to early morning and late evening. Another thing Mike had produced was a frying pan. About an hour after he had left one day Rob was using it to cook a pork chop he had brought him.

He also had some cold boiled potatoes which he chopped and tossed into the sizzling fat. He had not eaten since a piece of game pie at midday and was ravenously hungry. He knelt beside the stove, leaning forward both to watch the cooking and sniff the delicious smell. He heard a small sound outside the doorway. He was not as alert to this as he had been—he had developed a feeling of security bit by bit—but he looked up. If it had been Mike returning for some reason he would have heard his whistle. An animal? It might be. Then there was the unmistakable sound of a footfall and in the small flaring light of the stove's flame he could see that someone was standing outside, looking in at him.

He froze helplessly.

"So this is where Mike gets to," a voice said.

It was a woman's voice.

6

Questions at a Garden Party

She did not come in, but told Rob to switch off the stove and follow her outside. She stood in the clearing and watched him emerge from the bramble thicket.

It had been a fine day and some brightness lingered. He could see that she was about forty, of average height, with dark hair and dark eyes. She wore a coat and skirt of heavy-looking brown material and plain, flat shoes. She had a flimsy scarlet scarf at her neck and several rings on her fingers, one of them with a large blue stone.

"I'm Mike's mother. I'd like to know what this is all about."

Her voice had a slightly harsh quality. She sounded like a person used to having her questions answered, and promptly.

"I've just been living here," Rob said. "I haven't done anything."

Her eyes were studying him. He realized how scruffy he probably looked and felt ashamed.

"I want to know why," she said. "Who you are, where you come from."

He told her awkwardly, stumbling over the account. She listened, not interrupting or helping him when he was in difficulties. At the end she said, "And then?"

"I don't understand."

"What was to come next? You didn't expect to live out your days in a hole in the ground, did you?"

"We hadn't really planned."

She gave a small sigh of exasperation. "No, I suppose not. I think I'd better have a talk with Mike."

"He doesn't know . . . ?"

"About my coming here? No."

Mike had not betrayed him. He was ashamed of thinking he might have done.

"How did you find out?"

"Mike has been ill. Did he tell you?" Rob nodded. "We were advised to keep an eye on him. And he's been doing odd things—going out more and staying out longer. Then there was the matter of articles missing from the house. Food in particular. Households are better organized than you and he probably imagine. The housekeeper is accountable to me, the cook to the housekeeper, the kitchen maids to the cook. Feeding an extra mouth leaves traces."

"I'm sorry."

"There's no need. I'm telling you how I realized there was someone else on the scene. He always came in this direction. Today I found Captain tethered down by the river.

If you were concealing someone, this place would be as likely as any."

"You knew about it? Mike said he found it. It was all overgrown."

"It would be, after more than twenty years. I used to come here as a girl—Mike's father and I were cousins. We found it then." She gazed at the brambles as though recalling that distant time. "We even camped out in it, I remember."

Talking like this she was slightly less intimidating. But she turned back to him, frowning.

"We still have to decide what to do about you. It might be best for you to come back home with me now."

"I'm all right here. Really."

She was silent for a moment, undecided.

"I suppose if you've been here as long as this one more night will not make much difference. I'll come and see you again in the morning. Will you be warm enough?"

"Mike brought some blankets."

"Yes, I know. Are there enough?" Rob nodded. "Then I'll let you get back to your supper. What was it you were cooking? It smelled like pork."

"A chop."

"Then be sure you cook it properly. You must not take chances with pork. Good night, Rob."

Rob thought about what he should do. His chief impulse was to get away while he had the chance. He could be miles from here by the time she returned. He was better equipped than he had been for living rough, not only physically and mentally but with the different things Mike had given him. The knife alone would make a tremendous difference. It was better to go on the run again than to wait here for the inevitable. She had said things could not go on like this—an adult was bound to look at it in that way—and the obvious alternative was to send him back to the Conurb.

It was the thought of Mike which held him back. He had come to depend on him, and not just for material help. He wanted to talk to him about it. The idea crossed his mind of going up to the house, somehow getting in and finding him. That was impractical, though. He would almost certainly get caught which would only make matters worse. And even if he were not, he would never find Mike's room in a house that had so many.

His uncertainty was decided by the weather. He went into the clearing after supper and found that a drizzle of rain had started. When he looked again later it was much heavier, a drenching downpour. He retired to his lamplit cell, and to bed. If he were to make a break he could do so in the morning.

But in the morning the rain was coming down steadily and looked as though it had been doing so all night. The brambles scattered droplets down on him when he pulled them aside and everything outside—the clearing and the wood—was soaked and dripping. He went back in, dispirited and uncertain. He still had time to get clear because it was unlikely that anyone would come up from the house until the rain stopped. But if he did get away, what object could he have? He might be better fitted for living rough but he was also more conscious of the drawbacks. There was not much future, as Mike's mother had pointed out, in living in a hole in the ground.

After a couple of hours the rain stopped, and soon after there was blue in the sky. Rob took his things and went up to the stream to wash. There was a sheltered spot with a shelf of flat rock overlooking a pool. He was coming back when he heard Mike's whistle. He stopped, and heard it again. He had to make up his mind. He went forward slowly and into the clearing. The sun had broken through and the grass was beginning to steam with heat. Mike was there, his mother with him.

"You're still here? I wasn't sure if you would be," Mike said.

Rob wondered if there was a touch of disappointment in his voice. It would have solved a problem for Mike, too, if he had left during the night. He nodded.

"I'm still here."

"We need to talk," Mike's mother said.

Her face, in the full light of day, was more wrinkled than he had thought. It was a strong face, with deep eyes set close to a long straight nose. She had a mole on her right cheek. She was wearing a costume something like the one she had worn the previous day, but in a heathery-blue color. The scent she was wearing teased his nostrils.

"This isn't going to be easy," she continued.

Her eyes studied him and her voice with its slight harshness labeled him a nuisance. He glanced toward Mike who looked at him noncommittally. Rob said, trying to keep the resentment out of his voice, "It's all right. I can move on."

"Move on where?"

"Somewhere. I'll manage."

"You're only a boy," she said. "I doubt if you're Mike's age. And there is nowhere to go, anyway. We live in a civilized world and people have to fit in. The best thing would be to go back to the place you came from, to the Conurb."

Rob shook his head. "No."

"I thought of reporting you," she said. "For your own good. You have had troubles over there. Everyone does, everywhere. You would settle down and get used to things. We all have to adjust."

He was silent. He ought to have gone while he had the chance, but as long as she had not reported him yet there was hope. If he could persuade her not to do anything for a few days, a few hours even . . .

"I want to ask you again: will you do it—go back voluntarily?"

"No, not voluntarily."

She gave a small shrug. "Well, that's that. Mike and I have had a talk about you. An argument, in fact." She looked at her son with a faint smile. "He takes you very seriously and he wants to help you. The question is: how?"

He wondered about the argument; she did not seem like a person who would yield easily. He remembered the illness Mike had had, and what he had said about brain fever. She might be indulging him deliberately—might have been told to. Not that there was anything wrong with Mike's brain as far as he could see.

"If I could stay here for a little while . . ." he said.

"There is no point in that," she said crisply. "We must have a proper solution. If you're not to go back to the Con-

urb then you must live in the County. We can't fit you in
among the servants—there would be too many questions
asked. So we're left with fitting you into the family.''

"But I'm not . . .''

"You're not gentry, and there are a number of ways in
which it shows. Your speech, for instance. And we have to
be able to account for your origins and background. You
need to have a story that makes sense but is difficult if not
impossible to check. I think you will have to be a distant
cousin, a very distant cousin.''

He was impressed by the assurance with which she spoke.
It was fantastic but he had a feeling that it could work, if
she said so.

"Your coloring is dark,'' she continued. "You could pass
for someone who has lived in the East. The son, for instance, of a cousin of mine in Nepal, whom she has decided
to send to school in England following her husband's death.
Nepal would do very well. The king has discouraged West-
ern visitors and settlers for many years, and those Europeans
who live there are largely out of touch with home. Any
small errors in speech or manners would be assumed to be
due to that.''

"Do you have a cousin?'' Rob asked. "A real person?''

"When you address a lady,'' she said, "you say 'ma'am.'
That's probably true even in Nepal.''

He felt himself coloring. "I'm sorry, . . . ma'am.''

"Better. Yes, I do have a cousin there. Her name is
Amanda and her husband did die last year. She has no chil-
dren but no one here knows that. You had better keep your
Christian name, but you will be Rob Perrott, not Randall.''

"Yes," he said. "Yes, ma'am."

"Mike's father has been told the full story of course, and has given his approval. But we shan't take Cecily into our confidence. She is young and might say something wrong without meaning to."

"It's going to be a lot of trouble for you."

She did not deny it, but said, "You can make it easier by learning things quickly. There will be a lot to learn."

Rob was supposed to have come from Nepal to London Airport, and from there to the copter station at a small town fifteen miles away. The subterfuge was necessary, Mrs. Gifford explained, because of the servants who would naturally be curious about the new arrival. Mike would take him to the station and the Giffords would pick him up in the carriage.

Mike brought up two horses and they rode together across country. It was for Rob an uneasy and uncomfortable journey. The second horse according to Mike was an elderly hack with no spirit at all but he found it alarming all the same. Mike gave him advice and criticism which did not help a lot. He realized that he was going to have to learn horse riding if he were to live in the County, and the thought was depressing.

He was feeling altogether more depressed than seemed reasonable. He told himself how lucky he was. He had not been sent back to the Conurb, and was not having to live as a hunted fugitive. Instead he was being given a home, a background, a family. It was a staggering piece of good fortune.

But against this he had a sense of helplessness, of being

at the disposal of others. He was absolutely dependent on their charity and would have to fit in with their requirements. Mike was all right, but Mrs. Gifford scared him and the thought of a Mr. Gifford who had not even bothered to come up to the cave to see him was no more reassuring. He knew that although it had not been stated, he was on probation. The whole thing might be a trick, intended to last only as long as Mike was away from school. When Mike went back the Giffords might simply hand him over to the police.

The copter station was not actually in the town but near it. Copters seemed to emerge from and disappear into a green empty field. Mike explained that the station had been built in an artificial hollow so that it would not spoil the landscape. Landscapes were taken very seriously in the County. A small grove to one side concealed the place where carriages waited, and they tethered the horses there before going down a curving ramp. The landing field was circular, about a hundred yards across, with covered sides. There were service pits for the copters, waiting rooms, an inn, a coffee shop and a shop selling small articles for the traveler. People sat on cushioned benches or strolled about, the women in long dresses, the men in tight-fitting dark suits.

"That's the washroom where you can tidy yourself up," Mike said. "I'll leave now. Mother and Father will be along in about half an hour. I'll take the horses and hack home. All right?"

Rob nodded. "Fine."

The washroom had a white-haired attendant in a gray uniform with silver buttons, who showed him to a cubicle.

There was a lot of dark wood and gleaming mirrors, and a marble basin into which water gushed steaming from flaring brass taps. Rob washed and brushed himself. His reflection looked at him from the mirror. The clothes he had been given were a fairly good fit. Drab compared with dress in the Conurb, the only brightness in his case a green bow tie, but the cloth had a richer, more expensive feel to it.

He felt funny giving the attendant the tip Mike had specified, and stranger still when the old man, accepting it, touched his peaked cap. He supposed he would get used to this sort of thing eventually. He went out to wait for the arrival of the Giffords.

The house was even more impressive inside than out. There was so much space, so many rooms, such expanses of polished wood floor. All the furniture looked hundreds of years old and Mike told him that most of it was. There were skilled craftsmen in the County who made painstaking copies of old styles but much of what there was here had come down in the family from its original period. The walls, instead of being plastisprayed in colored patterns were covered with decorated embossed papers, with surfaces that were silky to the touch. There were displays of flowers in bowls or vases—not synthetic but real, cut in the garden and arranged each morning by Mrs. Gifford. Paintings hung in ornate frames that showed a dull gold, many portraits of men and women in ancient dress. Mike's ancestors, he realized.

There appeared to be an endless number of bedrooms leading off the first-floor landing. He was given one next to Mike's, sharing a bathroom with him. It was pleasantly and simply furnished and looked across the lawns to the river. It had an open grate and a wood fire was burning there when he was shown in by a servant. It crackled, spitting occasionally, and had a tangy smoky smell. He was standing looking at it when Mike knocked and came in.

"Everything all right?" he asked.

"Yes." Rob pointed to the lumoglobe on the wall above the bed. "I thought you used oil lamps?"

"We do, downstairs. Not in the bedrooms. Not in the servants' quarters, either."

"Why?"

"Well . . . everyone does. It's customary."

"Customary," Rob was to learn, was a word much used and generally accepted as unquestionable. But now he asked:

"Why the mixture? Why not have everything old-fashioned, or everything modern?"

Mike hesitated. "I've never really thought about it. As I say, it's customary. Some things are used, some not. Take machines. There's the road layer, and farmers use machines in the fields. The servants have electrical gadgets to help with cleaning and all that. My father uses an electric shaver, though some men—most probably—shave with soap and water. There's no hard and fast rule. You just—well, you know what's suitable."

"What about holovision?"

Mike made a face. "Good God, no!" He put a hand on Rob's shoulder. "You'll soon get the hang of it."

Mr. Gifford was a taciturn, rather awesome figure. When he spoke it was in a clipped fashion which Rob thought at first indicated disapproval. He tried to keep out of his way as much as possible. This was made easier by the fact that Mr. Gifford spent a great deal of time in the conservatory pursuing his hobby: the growing and cultivation of miniature trees.

About a week after his arrival Rob found the conservatory empty and ventured inside. Mike was with the family doctor who had arrived, his bag strapped to the saddle of a magnificent black horse, to give him a checkup. There were rows of shelves with little trees in pots and also a Lilliputian landscape with a stream running through a forest of oak and fir, maple and beech and elm, to a lake where tiny weeping willows trailed their leaves in the water.

The running stream in particular was fascinating. Rob could hear a faint hum and confirmed his suspicion: the water was being kept in circulation by an electric pump. This must be another of the cases where technology was permitted to intrude. It was gradually beginning to make a sort of sense. Gadgets must be kept to the bedroom and bathroom and the servants' quarter. Where they were allowed into the house proper they had to be for some special purpose which was regarded as suitable. Such as landscaping in miniature. He heard the door open behind him and turned in alarm to see Mr. Gifford coming in.

"I haven't touched anything, sir. I was just looking," Mike explained.

"Are you interested in bonsai?" Mr. Gifford asked.

"Do you mean these trees? Yes, but I've never seen anything like them before."

It was enough to set Mr. Gifford off. Reticence disappeared; his speech was clipped still but tumbling over itself in explanation and demonstration. It had not, Rob realized, been disapproval so much as shyness. He showed him the different methods of propagation: from seed, from cuttings, or by layering. Seeding was the best method, but the slowest. You never got the same elegance of root shape with the other forms. The root was the key to good bonsai. You had to trim them with great care in winter when you repotted the tree. Then there was pinching and pruning—always the former for preference rather than the latter. A bud pinched out gently by thumb and forefinger or with small blunt forceps left no mark. When you pruned there was a stump which marred the natural elegance of the tree.

Then there was training. When the sap was running you could either bend or straighten the branches or the trunk by staking or weighting them, or by anchoring them to stiff wires. When you put weight on to depress a branch, you needed a counterweight on the other side of the trunk to prevent the roots from lifting. He showed Rob an oak with a split trunk, dropping down on either side of its pot.

"Only five years old." He shook his head. "I don't do much of that sort of thing—forced trailing. Unnatural, I always think. Now, this is different."

He led the way across the room. Mr. Gifford pointed to the artificial landscape. "See the brow of the hill? I've assumed a prevailing wind. Westerly. Catches the trees just there. You see they're all windswept? All leaning the same way. Of course they've never been in a wind, a breeze even. That's all done by pot training."

"It's very realistic."

"Isn't it! Isn't it? I'm glad you're so interested. Come in here whenever you like. You can do some of your own if you want to."

Rob thanked him.

"Layering's best if you want something to show early," Mr. Gifford said. "You young people are all impatient. Chinese layering's very easy. Instead of taking the branch down to the soil you take the soil up to the branch. Find a shapely tip of tree, cut a strip of bark all around where you want it to root, and tie a pack of wet sphagnum moss and compost around it. May take a year or two for roots to form, but you'll get a tree which would take ten or more to raise from seed. This one here . . ."

There was no difficulty in getting on with Mike's sister, Cecily. She was eleven, a slim dark girl, resembling Mike only in the blueness of her eyes. She was a great talker—to the family, the servants, the various cats and dogs that wandered in and out of the house. She had a pleasant voice, high and musical. It was her curiosity Rob found a bit trying. She was delighted with her new cousin but also intrigued. She wanted to know everything about him. Mrs. Gifford chided her for asking personal questions but Rob could see, from the rebellious look in her eyes, that this was not going to have any permanent effect. Eventually she would get him on his own and try again.

He found help in the library. This was a room about fifteen feet by twenty-five, its walls almost completely lined with glass-fronted cases that reached up nearly to the high ceiling patterned with rosettes. The cases were full of books, nearly all bound in leather. There were thousands—more than the entire stock of the Public Library, and all for the use of one small family.

At the moment, he realized with a mixture of surprise and satisfaction, for his own personal use. None of the family seemed to go there and he could browse without interruption. He did this particularly when Mike was occupied with his tutor, and sat for hours reading in an armchair by one of the tall pointed-arch windows.

The books were various but had one thing in common: none had been published within the last thirty or forty years. There was a great emphasis on country sports and activities—volume after volume on fly-fishing, hunting, and all aspects of the care and riding of horses. There was also a good concentration of ancient biography—memoirs of the landed gentry and of those who had lived abroad in the days of the colonies. This gave Rob an idea and he searched for works dealing with Nepal. He found several and read them carefully, making mental notes. When Cecily cornered him, he was ready for her.

The references were all at least half a century out of date, some twice that, but according to Mrs. Gifford it was a part of the world whose rulers had chosen to keep primitive so one could hope that there had been not much change. Rob told her about the villages clinging to the sides of hills, themselves overshadowed by the snowy majesty of the peaks of the Himalayas. He spoke of oxen ploughing the stony fields and the shaggy yak which really came from Tibet, of spring when all manner of flowers—scarlet poinsettia, mauve ageratum, trumpet-flowered datura—burst forth from the earth and bloomed, of the burning summers and the freezing winters.

Cecily clapped her hands in delight. "How wonderful!" she said. "How could you bear to leave it?"

Later Mike said, grinning, "That must have been a very impressive account you gave Ciss of life in the East. She insisted on telling it all to me—what she could remember."

"I may have overdone it a bit."

"You convinced her, anyway. Did you make it all up?"

He told him about the books he had found. Mike nodded. "A good idea, that."

"Why aren't there any recent books?" Rob asked. "I know books are no longer printed in the Conurbs, but surely it's different here? I mean, you have private libraries."

"I should think enough have been published already. You'd need a lifetime to read them. And there are so many other things to do. We probably don't want any more."

"Does no one write books now?"

"Not books as such. Some people write essays, poems, that sort of thing." He spoke with tolerant lack of interest. "They produce them privately, just a few copies for friends. Handwritten, a lot of them. Very pretty to look at."

He got on all right with Mr. Gifford and Cecily and of course Mike, less well with Mrs. Gifford and the servants. In some ways the servants made him more uneasy than she did. He could not come to terms with their deference and had the feeling that they were laughing at him behind his back, even that they guessed the truth and were biding their time before reporting him.

There was Harry, for instance, the head groom. He had taken charge of Rob's lessons in horse riding, accepting his complete lack of ability without a query or demur. He was a harsh taskmaster, relentlessly drawing attention to faults and weaknesses. His tone in the paddock was stern and sometimes angry. Rob resented it even when he knew it was justified. And he was baffled by the change which took place outside, by being called "Master Rob" and saluted with hand to forelock by this little bandy-legged man who was older than his father had been. Mike obviously saw nothing strange, no conflict between the two attitudes, but Rob could not understand it.

Mrs. Gifford, too, was a formidable proposition. She treated him with every sign of kindness but he could not be sure of her. He had come to realize that hers was the really important influence—respect was paid to Mr. Gifford as head of the house but he left all decisions in her hands— and he did not know what she would eventually decide about him. What perhaps she already had decided, but kept concealed behind the unbroken façade of calm good manners.

She gave him a part of her time every day to coach him in the way he was required to behave. There was an awful lot of this—how to address ladies, how to enter a room, how to walk or stand or bow, how to eat and drink, what sort of things to say in polite conversation and what must not be said. She corrected his mistakes and pointed out things he had done wrong during the previous day, not with the roughness and anger of the groom but with a cool decisiveness that could be even more disconcerting. At times, when she smiled and praised him for something, he thought she liked him; at others he was sure she detested him as a nuisance. He came to dread the visits to the little parlor where she sat over her embroidery, yet also in an odd way to look forward to them. When she did praise him it was exhilarating.

She told him one evening that he had been accepted for entry to the school to which Mike also would return in the autumn.

"Do I have to go, Aunt Margaret?"

"Of course. That is the reason we have given for your being sent back from Nepal."

He had forgotten that. He was silent, thinking about it. Another way of life to get used to: more and more problems. There was no end to them.

As though reading his thoughts, Mrs. Gifford said, "You must not expect it to be easy, Rob. If you are to pass as one of us you are going to have to work very hard at it. Very hard indeed."

He had been introduced to a number of people—neighbors, the family doctor, the vet when he called to see a lame horse—and had got by. He had been nervous, but either Mike or Mrs. Gifford had been at hand to help him. There was a more severe ordeal when he had been with the family three weeks: the Giffords gave a garden party.

Giving and receiving hospitality was one of the main occupations of the gentry. There had already been several evening functions—for drinks or supper—which he and Mike were left out of on account of age. Garden parties,

though, were afternoon occasions, with children present
and the beverages nonalcoholic. There would be more than
two hundred guests for this one.

It was to be held out of doors if possible. There had been
several days of cold cloudiness and intermittent blowing
rain but it cleared and the day was fine. A marquee had been
set up on the lawn, and carriages began rolling up the drive
just before three.

Rob stood with the family and was introduced to guests
as they arrived. They were all elegantly dressed. The ladies
wore flowing silk and chiffon gowns with big gay fantastic
hats, the men tail-jacketed suits, gray top hats, and flowers
in their buttonholes. Mrs. Gifford gave him quiet instruc-
tion on people as they approached, and he bowed and shook
hands with them as he had been taught, and made brief
smiling replies to their comments.

After the reception he was released from duty but had to
stay and mingle with the crowd. A small gymkhana was held
in the paddock, where jumps had been put up, and he
watched Mike take fourth place on Captain. He was jump-
ing against men and his round was greeted with applause.
He doffed his riding cap in response. Watching, Rob envied
him—not the success but the fact of belonging so completely. However much he learned and copied, he knew he
would always be outside this world, a stranger.

People drifted away from the paddock in the direction of
the refreshment marquee and Rob went with them. There
would be other sports later: archery and canoeing on the
river. He was thinking of lemonade, made, unlike that in
the Conurbs, with real lemons, when he was hailed.

There were two men, one middle aged, the other quite old. It was the first of these, a squat powerful figure with a curling moustache and a deep cleft in his chin who had called his name, and Rob recognized him. Mrs. Gifford had identified him as Sir Percy Gregory, Lord Lieutenant of the county and an important figure. The other man, taller and white haired, he vaguely remembered as one of a group that had passed down the line. Rob made a small bow, and said, "Did you want me, sir?"

"This is the lad, Harcourt." Sir Percy nodded to his companion. "Maggie Gifford's cousin's boy."

Harcourt nodded also. He had small sharp eyes behind gold-rimmed spectacles: contact lenses for men was another thing not customary in the County.

"From Nepal, Sir Percy tells me. It's a small world. I lived out there for a time myself as a young man." He smiled wintrily. "That's a few years ago, of course."

Rob hoped he was not showing his dismay. He looked for Mrs. Gifford but there was no sign of her. He realized the two men were watching him and tried to smile.

"It's a big country, of course," Harcourt said. "Over fifty thousand square miles."

"Yes, sir," Rob said gratefully.

The relief was short lived.

"Which is your neighborhood?" Harcourt asked.

He thought desperately of the most detailed of the books he had read, unfortunately not the most recent, and said:

"Katmandu."

"I was a year there," Harcourt said. "Do you know the Dennings?"

Rob made the swift decision that it was safer to deny than affirm an acquaintance which could lead to more, and more difficult questions. He felt it was the wrong one, though, when Harcourt's brow furrowed and he said, "Odd. They've lived there a couple of hundred years."

Harcourt went on talking about Katmandu, occasionally putting queries which Rob dealt with as best he could. He had the sinking feeling that his best was not very good. Harcourt's tone seemed critical, and he thought Sir Percy looked at him in a probing doubtful way. He became confused and stammered over his answers.

"Notice anything about the way he speaks—his accent?" Harcourt said.

"There's something unusual," Sir Percy replied.

Rob braced himself. It had been foolish to think he could get away with it. He wondered if they would send police to take him now or wait until after the garden party.

"Very unusual," Harcourt said. He gave a little crow of laughter. "Typical Nepalese settler twang. Old Dumbo Denning spoke just the same way. I suppose he's dead, and that boy of his pushed off somewhere." He shook his head. "People get forgotten."

"That's true," Sir Percy said. He gave Rob a nod of dismissal. "Let's go and see if we can find a cup of tea."

7

The Revolutionaries

It was a good summer. Day after day came blue and hot, the mornings occasionally misty but the sun breaking clear after an hour or two and scorching through the afternoon to a calm warm sunset. Once or twice clouds built up and there was rolling thunder, brief torrential rain, and the land washed clean and brilliant. No one under fifty could remember a season as fine, and even the older ones admitted it compared well with the dazzling summers of their youth.

There were plenty of things to do. Rob had a horse of his own, a dapple-gray mare called Sonnet, and he ranged the countryside on it with Mike. Almost every week there was a show somewhere, with flowers, fruit and vegetables, all carefully hand grown, arranged for judging in long tents heavy with the mixture of their fragrances. There was always a riding event, as well. Rob did not enter for these—he had learned to ride adequately but with no special skill—but watched Mike carry off several prizes. Then there was a regatta, held on the river near Oxford, with individual sculling and various team events including the bump races in which boats started at timed intervals and eliminated each other by closing the gap in front. There was cricket, a game forgotten in the Conurb but whose slowness and formality and restfulness seemed well suited to the life of the County and to the succession of hot summer days. There were fairs and parties.

One party centered on the major archery contest of the year. It was held nearly twenty miles from Gifford House, and Mike and Rob rode over the day before and slept in a tented camp that had been put up in the park of Old Hall. This was the home of the Lord Lieutenant, Sir Percy Gregory, the sponsor of the contest, himself a keen archer.

It was a sport that Rob found he particularly enjoyed. Mike beat him, as he did in everything, but the margin was not so great. Rob said, in the morning, that he thought of entering in their age group. Mike looked surprised but said, "Why not? A good idea, really."

The suggestion had been made on impulse and Rob later was inclined to withdraw it. Quite apart from his lack of skill, it seemed wiser to keep in the background. He was accepted as Mike's cousin from the East but there was no point in drawing attention to himself unnecessarily. He voiced his doubts to Mike, who disagreed.

"More conspicuous if you don't go in for anything, I should think. There'll be a whole mob competing."

There were six heats before the final and Mike and Rob

were not drawn together. Mike came in second in his heat, Rob third in his, barely qualifying by a single point over the boy in fourth place.

But he had been improving all the time. In the final his eye was in and he felt relaxed. He wound up with a couple of golds, which raised applause. He finished third in the event. Mike, shooting later, was erratic and came eleventh.

Sir Percy presented Rob with a small silver medal.

"Nice shooting, boy," he said. "You stand well. I suppose you've done quite a bit of archery out in Nepal?"

It would have been nice to be able to say that he had never seen a bow or arrows until three months ago.

"A bit, sir."

"Keep it up. You've the makings of a bowman."

Mike congratulated him heartily enough. Later, though, he returned to the subject in a slightly different mood. He was not carping or resentful, more bewildered. He did not put it like that but he was plainly surprised that Rob should have beaten him—should beat him in anything. The pupil had surpassed the instructor and it puzzled him. It occurred to Rob that the whole enterprise—of taking in the fugitive boy from the Conurb and passing him off as gentry—had been a sort of sport to Mike; and he had thought of Rob as an object in the sport rather than as a person in his own right. Now, through having to give best to him in this one small thing, he was being forced to look at him differently, with respect even.

Rob resented this a bit. If he had thought about it he would have expected Mike to regard himself as superior, but it was not something he had thought about. Nor wanted to now. And yet it was better in the open—and he *had* beaten him at archery. He had shown he was not just someone to be helped, on a whim.

That evening, as they lay in their tent in the dusk, watching the bats swoop across the sky outside, Mike asked Rob questions. They were questions about his earlier life, about the Conurb. It was something he had not done before. Like everyone else in the County he knew a little about the Conurb: enough to be contemptuous of it. It was the place of the mob, where people dashed around in electrocars, crowded together like sardines, listened to raucous pop music, watched holovision and the bloodthirsty Games—for the most part watched the Games *on* holovision. It was the place where everyone ate processed foods and liked them, where there were riots and civil disturbances, where no one knew how to behave properly, how to dress or exchange courtesies, how to speak English even. It was the place one knew existed and, apart from thanking God one did not have to live there, preferred to forget.

The questions were particular rather than general—about Rob's family, people he had known, the boys at school. Of Rob's father, he said, "After your mother,died he must have been lonely."

"I suppose so."

"I wonder if he ever wanted to come over to the County? He had been here, when he met your mother."

It was something that had not occurred to Rob. It could be true. He had imagined his mother pining for the life she had known as a girl, but his father had experienced it too, even though briefly. When she died, and afterward, he must have thought about those days, and wished them back.

"There's no interchange at all now," Mike said, "apart from the Commuters. Conurbans are not allowed to come into the County. Why is that?"

"They don't want to come."

"You did."

Rob could hardly say he was different from the rest. Immodesty, by the standards of the County, was one of the deadlier sins. "If they did come they would make a pretty unpleasant mess of things, wouldn't they? Sixty millions of them . . . with holiday camps and electrocars and community singing and riots when they got drunk . . ."

"Not all of them, of course. A few, perhaps."

"There's no such thing as a few in the Conurbs," Rob said. "They aren't happy unless they're all doing the same thing at the same time."

He surprised himself by the intensity with which he said that. He reminded himself that he had lived in the Conurb and had not been, until his father's death, unhappy there. He had not realized how accustomed he had grown to this easier and more luxurious life until Mike's questions recalled the old one.

"That's what I've always thought," Mike said, "but is it true? The people you've been talking about—they don't sound all that different from people here. Might there not be some who would like to live in another way but don't know how to set about it? Like your father, perhaps."

Rob rolled over in the sleeping bag which had been

bought for him for this trip. It was identical with the one Mike had. The glow of satisfaction that remained from his archery success was mixed with a pleasant tiredness.

"Nothing anyone can do about it, anyway," he said, yawning.

"I suppose not," Mike replied. "All the same . . ."

Rob drifted into sleep.

They went to school together in September. It centered around an ancient abbey which had ceased to be a religious foundation at the time of Henry VIII but kept many of the original features including a Gothic chapel with very old stained glass in the windows. Boarding houses and other necessary departments which had been built nearby harmonized with it. They were no more than fifty years old but looked five hundred. The group stood in a quiet valley in green rolling country, with a view on clear days of the distant Welsh mountains.

The school had come to its present position from what was now a part of the Conurb, and boarding houses were named after landmarks in the old city. There were Cathedral, Westgate, Itchen, St. Cross, Chesil, and one simply called College in which Rob joined Mike.

He was apprehensive and uneasy at the beginning, but it was not as bad as he had expected. Life was arduous, but tolerable and in some ways enjoyable. They were awakened even earlier than at the boarding school and went out, in all weathers, for a two-mile run, dressed only in shorts and running shoes. Returning, they showered in stinging cold water. This was followed by an hour and a half of lessons before breakfast, by which time they were all ravenously hungry.

The day was filled with lessons and duties, and infringements of discipline were sharply punished, often by beating with canes. In some ways discipline was more severe here because there were a thousand minor rules you could break, not always realizing you were doing so. There were certain liberties of dress and behavior which went by seniority. At the junior level life followed complicated paths and patterns.

The difference between the two places was not easy to grasp at first, but it was distinct. Gradually Rob worked it out as having to do with pride and self-respect. At the boarding school there had been nothing to make up for the hardships. The whole aim had been to grind you down to submissiveness. Here there was a sense of being trained, and trained for eventual authority. This was shown over meals, for example. When, after the run and the cold shower and the early morning lessons, the boys went into the dining room for breakfast they had to sit on hard wooden benches. The food, though ample and well cooked, was plain. But it was brought to the tables by servant girls. They belonged to a special, privileged group, and this was never allowed to be forgotten.

Mike did his best to help Rob fit in with things, but a lot had to be learned by experience. The habit Rob had formed during his months with the Giffords of watching people, anticipating things they might do or say and being ready to respond, proved an advantage. He worked out the right procedures and did his best to follow them. Quite soon he found himself fitting in, accepting and being accepted. At the beginning some of the boys asked him questions about Nepal but he had no difficulty in coping with them and after a time they stopped. He made friends apart from Mike: they were in different classes for most things.

Games were important. They played a different kind of football from that in the Conurb: the ball was oval instead of round and you were allowed to pick it up and run with it. It was a rougher, more bruising game, and Rob found he could play quite well. Mike and he were both picked for the first junior house match after a few weeks, Mike as a forward and Rob in the more prominent position of wing three-quarter. It was a hard game which their side won. Afterward they walked back across the muddy field together in the direction of the changing rooms. Rob was talking about the match and Mike made abstracted responses. Then he said,

"You played football in the Conurb, didn't you? What they call soccer?"

Rob glanced around quickly but there was no one near.

"Yes. I like this better."

"It's a funny thing . . . Did you know that in the old days, when the school was inside what's now the Conurb, we played soccer? Most public schools played rugby but we didn't."

"Really?" Rob said, but without much interest.

"Why the change?"

"Does it matter?"

"It was a school tradition and you know what this place is like about traditions. It changed that one though. Because soccer is a Conurb game and we musn't do anything the same as they do?"

Rob shrugged. "I suppose it could be."

"But why? Why do all these differences have to be created and maintained?"

They walked on in silence. Mike had periods of moodiness and Rob had discovered it was better to pay as little attention to them as possible. Increasingly, since the day of the archery contest, they had involved questionings and criticisms of things which no one, Rob felt, could do anything about. It was not that the present mood seemed unfriendly. If anything there was a feeling of closeness, as though Mike were letting him in on an important part of himself, of the way he thought.

Mike said abruptly, "You know Penfold?"

Rob knew him by sight. He was a senior boy, in his final year; not a prefect though one would have thought that he ought to have been. He was tall and lanky, with an ugly but distinctive face. He had been good at games but had stopped playing them. He had also won an Oxford scholarship.

"Yes," Rob said.

"He was telling me about it. There's a group of chaps who meet in his study and talk. Do you feel like coming along after supper?"

Rob hesitated. It was not just that Penfold was odd, thought by both masters and boys to be in some way unreliable. It was also true that juniors were not encouraged to mix with senior boys. They would not be breaking an actual rule but it meant going against custom and one did not do that lightly. On the other hand he could hardly refuse the suggestion when Mike put it this way.

"All right," he said. "If you like."

Penfold's study was about eight feet square, bare except for bed, small wardrobe, table and single chair. Ten boys crowded it badly. Some sat on the bed, others on the floor or leaning against the wall. Penfold himself sat on the window ledge looking in to them. He spoke in a rapid, slightly hectoring voice.

"The point we have to start from is the realization that we're all conditioned—that we live in the most conditioned society the world has ever known. We have our special position drilled into us from childhood. The servants here in the county are taught to despise the Conurbans and the Conurbans despise them in return. They never meet—they each know scarcely anything about the way the other lives —but they despise them all the same. And we are the privileged ones at the top of the pyramid.

"The actual difference in classes is not new. There always have been a privileged few and an unprivileged mass, and there have always been people willing to accept a position as servants of the few and think themselves lucky on account of it. But now we have an absolute division: gentry and their servants on the one hand, Conurbans on the other. The Commuters regard themselves as gentry and look forward to the time when they can retire inside the County and not have to go back to the Conurbs. There are two worlds, with a barrier between them. The barrier may not be strong in the physical sense but in people's minds it's enormous. We the rulers and they the ruled, and never the twain shall meet."

A boy called Logan who was almost as old as Penfold asked, "What do you want us to do about it?"

"Change it," Penfold said.

"Just like that?" Logan laughed. "Tall order."

"There are two ways in which societies can be changed," Penfold said. "If the masses are badly enough treated they may be forced into some kind of revolt. That's the desperate way and there's not much chance of it happening at present. The Conurbans aren't starved or ill treated. They get their bread and circuses like the citizens of Rome used to in the days of the Roman Empire. And there's butter and jam on the bread and you can see the circuses without stirring from your armchair, 3-D on holovision. The Conurbans won't start any revolutions."

Someone said, "They have riots, don't they?"

"So I believe. Safety valves to let off steam, and police enough to handle them comfortably. It's all cleverly worked out. Like the life we lead here in the County. We don't have holovision. That's for the vulgar lower classes, for the Conurbans who don't know how to occupy their empty lives. Or is it because we and they mustn't be allowed to share anything? As far as we're concerned the clock stopped just before the sun went down on the British Empire. We'll go on living forever in the afternoon glow—with horses and carriages, servants by the dozen, ladies in silk dresses and port and cigars after dinner."

He spoke with scathing contempt. A boy called Rowlands said, "Don't see much wrong with it."

"Don't you?"

Logan said, "You spoke of two ways of changing things. What's the other?"

"It's always been the more effective one," Penfold said. "It's done by the people inside the ruling class who realize that the system is rotten. They get together and do something about it."

"Such as?"

"Persuading. Agitating." Penfold paused. "Using force if necessary."

"How do we start?" Rowlands asked. "By hanging the Head Man from the flagpost?"

The reference to the headmaster caused some amusement. Rob wondered if any of those present took Penfold seriously in the smallest degree. It was, of course, quite ludicrous to think of schoolboys going out and starting a revolution.

"We start by preparing ourselves," Penfold said. His voice sounded strained. "There are others who think the same way. Older people."

"Do you know any?"

Penfold hesitated. "Yes."

"Well, who?"

He stared around the crowded room. "I don't want to say at this stage."

There was another ripple of scornful laughter. He had lost them, Rob saw. Most of them, at least. He noticed Mike had not been laughing.

Logan said, "What it seems to boil down to is this: ninety-nine percent or more are happy with the way things are. The Conurbans are happy, the Commuters are happy, our servants are happy, and most of us aren't complaining. You want us to go out and bust everything up. Why? So that we can go into the Conurbs? Hands up those who want crowds, street rioting and mass living in general. Not even you, Penfold? So that the Conurbans can come over here? With no holovision? They'd go mad inside a couple of days. All right, say it's true we're kept apart. We can't go there and they can't come here. But neither of us wants to. Are you going to launch a revolution to force us to do what we don't want to do?"

"You don't understand," Penfold said.

"Fair enough," Logan said. "You explain."

"I'm not saying most people aren't reasonably contented . . ."

"But you want them to be *dis*contented? Is that it?"

"In a way, yes."

A hoot of laughter made Penfold stop. It was several moments before he could go on. "Being discontented is a part of being free. And we aren't free—that's what I'm trying to say."

"Free to talk bilge," Rowlands said. "I've had enough of this lot."

Rob and Mike shared a study-bedroom. They did not say much on the way back. When they were inside, though, Mike said, "What did you think?"

"About Penfold? I wasn't all that impressed. What Rowlands said at the end made sense. Nobody stops him talking like that, so what's all this about people not being free?"

"They don't mind as long as it's only talk."

"They?"

"The government."

"Well, if it is only talk, what's the use of it?"

"If there were more than that . . ."

"What do you mean?"

"In confidence. All right?"

"Yes, of course."

"There are others, outside the school. Penfold's in touch with them. That thing tonight . . . it was just a blind, and a way of finding those who might be sympathetic. The real thing is different, a proper organization."

"Penfold told you this?" Mike nodded. "Do you believe him?"

"Yes. His brother's part of it. He's been out in the China War. He came back at the beginning of the year."

"It's still ridiculous," Rob said.

"You could find out."

"Find out what?"

"Whether it's ridiculous or not. By coming in. You'd have to take an oath of secrecy, of course."

He began to see that Mike was serious about this. The idea itself was nonsense but Mike believed in it. He hesitated, then said, "I don't think I would be much use."

"That's where you're wrong. You know the Conurb. There are all sorts of ways in which you could be useful. If for no other reason than because you would be demonstrating that Conurbans are people just like us, that the picture the gentry have of them as an ignorant mass, as sub-men almost, is quite wrong." He spoke earnestly. "You could help a lot, Rob."

"And if things don't work out—if it gets squashed? What then?"

Mike shrugged. "It's a chance we have to take."

"It's not quite the same chance, though, is it? The men might get sent to prison. They probably wouldn't bother with boys. Not if everything else was all right. But it's obvious what would happen to me: I'd be sent back to the Conurb."

Mike was silent. Rob was getting ready to say something else when Mike said,

"You're right. I hadn't thought of that. In your case it's too much to ask."

He was relieved that Mike had accepted it so easily. At the same time he felt guilty. Without Mike he would not be here, safe in the County. He could not have survived and escaped capture on his own. He started to argue, not about the particular point but about the whole idea. Since nearly everyone was satisfied it was lunatic to want to upset everything on the whim of a few. And even more lunatic to think there was any chance of a revolt succeeding. How could it?

Mike interrupted his thoughts, "Changes have been made by a few people before now, provided they were determined enough. Very big changes."

"Who, you and Penfold and Penfold's brother?" Rob said angrily.

"More than that."

"How many? Half a dozen?" Mike did not answer. "You must be crazy."

Mike shook his head. "I don't know." He climbed into bed. "Or everyone else is."

"Does that include me?"

Mike grinned across the room at him. "I suppose it has to. Never mind, you're in the majority. By the way, last in puts the light out."

8

Horsemen Riding Out

The term wore on, speeding faster toward its end. The last few weeks and days seemed to race by. There was the end-of-term concert, the end-of-term feast, and then it was a bright frosty morning and they were in the post coach rolling between fields carpeted with a light fall of snow, hearing the coachman's horn shiver in the clear cold air. At the market town the Giffords' carriage was waiting to take them through country, that winter could not make less familiar, to the river and the wood and at last the house itself, quiet and at peace in its parkland. Cecily came running out to meet them, with Mrs. Gifford coming more sedately after her. Even Mr. Gifford deserted his tiny trees to welcome them. They were home again.

Once again there was no shortage of things to do. The hunting season was in full swing and there was a local meet twice a week. In fact the Giffords belonged to several hunts. It was easy enough to get out four or five times in the week and by hacking a few miles more it was possible to manage every day except Sunday. Mr. Gifford did not hunt, but Mrs. Gifford did and even Cecily followed enthusiastically on her pony.

Rob found he enjoyed it also. He was nauseated at the first kill, when blood from the dead fox was rubbed on his face, but he realized it was something that had to be got through. It was customary; and custom ruled all. On the other side of the ledger there was the reward of new sights and sounds: huntsmen in the red jackets which were called pinks, the glossy sweet-smelling horses, hounds giving tongue as they swept in a checkered flood down a hillside, the horn's golden blast on a gray morning—the countryside itself from a hundred different vantage points. There was the exercise and the exhilaration—the warm tired glow at the end of the day jogging home toward a hot bath, toward tea and crumpets in front of a blazing fire with lamplight blooming softly in the room. There was the sense of belonging.

Christmas came, a time of feasting, of the giving and receiving of presents. A tree was set up in the hall, carrying gifts for every one of the servants down to the newest assistant to the head gardener, a shy awkward boy younger than Rob and Mike. The weather turned mild. The carriage took them to the village church through a shower of rain but came back in sunshine. There was turkey and flaming plum pudding with brandy butter, mince pies, nuts and wine, crackers with funny hats and ridiculous tokens and slips of paper printed with jokes so bad that everyone laughed at them uproariously.

On the surface it was not so different from Christmas in the Conurb. There, too, there had been turkey and pudding and crackers, and good cheer of a kind, but it was all a pale copy of what there was here. In the evening the carol singers came up from the village, first standing outside with their lanterns singing and then being summoned into the drawing room to sing again. Rob remembered the previous Christmas, and sitting watching the succession of Christmas parties on holovision. Even then they had seemed a little false; now the recollection made him shudder.

Later Cecily asked him, "Rob, what's Christmas like in Nepal?"

"Oh, pretty much the same."

She was lying on her stomach in front of the fire. Her dark hair showed one spot of gleaming bronze, reflecting the blaze. She pushed up on her elbows and stared at him.

"But there must be *some* differences."

"Well, little ones. Such as having roast dodo instead of turkey."

"But the dodo's extinct. I know that."

"Not in Nepal." He spoke lazily. Her questions no longer worried him. He could even tease her. "They live in these little valleys up in the mountains, eating lemons and ginger. It gives them a wonderful flavor."

"You're having me on," she said suspiciously.

"Not a bit. And then there are the Abominable Snowmen."

"I've heard about them. But why are they called abominable?"

"Because when they come to visit they take up all the fire just as you're doing. And then they melt and drip icy water all over the carpet. Wouldn't you call that pretty abominable?"

She got up and launched herself in an attack on him. Rob fended her off, laughing. Mrs. Gifford watched them for a few moments, smiling, and then said:

"Bedtime, darling."

"Mummy! It's Christmas."

"And that is why you have been allowed to stay up so late. Off now. I'll come and see you in ten minutes."

She frowned but made her good-bys and went, picking up a small lamp to light her way upstairs. Rob lay back, relaxing. There was a tinkle of music from the next room where Mike was playing the piano. Mr. Gifford had gone to give his trees their final check for the day.

"So you and Mike are off on January the second?" Mrs. Gifford said.

An invitation had come from the Penfolds to both boys, asking them to spend a few days there. Rob had not been particularly keen but it was obvious that Mike was, so he had resigned himself to it. "Yes, Aunt Margaret," he said and waited.

Mrs. Gifford was wearing her reading glasses, which made her look severe. But this, like the slight harshness of her voice, was misleading. She still made Rob feel uneasy at times but that was no longer because of any fear that she might abandon the experiment and have him sent away. He had learned that she was not a person who took things on lightly, or dropped them when they proved difficult. She had tremendous strength of mind and was formidably good at grasping and getting to the root of problems.

"It's Daniel Penfold who's at school with you, isn't it?" she asked.

"Was," Rob said. "He's left. He's going up to Oxford in the autumn."

The needle moved in the embroidery. "What's he like?"

"I don't know him very well."

"Not as well as Mike does?"

He said warily: "Well, I've only been at the school for one term."

"He's clever, I believe?"

To be described as clever was not, as Rob had discovered, a complimentary thing in the County. Most people who were clever did their best to disguise it. He said, "He got a Balliol scholarship."

"Yes." She nodded. "I'd heard he was clever."

She went on with her embroidery in silence. Rob was hoping this meant the conversation was over. It made him uncomfortable talking about Penfold to Mike's mother. When she did speak again, he was relieved that it seemed to be on a different tack.

"Your report was good, Rob."

"Thank you, Aunt Margaret."

"You are making very fair progress and you should be over the most difficult part. I wish I could say the same for Mike."

He made no reply to that. She held up a colored silk and bit it.

"His report was worrying. Too many phrases like 'can do better' and 'is not giving of his best.' In sport, too. As far as I remember, the games master said: 'He is not living up to his earlier promise, chiefly through lack of interest.' "

"He was ill last spring, wasn't he?" Rob said.

"That's nearly a year ago."

Rob was silent again. It was better to say too little than too much. Mrs. Gifford went on:

"And then there's this visit to the Penfolds. We don't know them very well, but what I've heard about the older boy is not particularly good. I gather his army record was —well, not entirely satisfactory. He resigned his commission but I believe he was under some pressure to do so."

Rob looked up and saw her eyes on him.

"I wouldn't normally talk to you in this strain, Rob." That was true. Gossip was a common pastime in the County but not one that Mrs. Gifford indulged in. "The reason I do so is because I am sure you want to help Mike in any way you can."

She did not say: remembering what he did for you. She did not have to. It was one of those moments in which the strength of her personality seemed to swamp him. He had an impulse to tell her everything, about Mike and Penfold and the scheme for starting a revolution. But no gentleman betrayed the trust of another. He could remember her saying that during one of those summer sessions in which she had instructed and coached him in the nuances of the way of life he was going to have to adopt. More even than actual consideration for Mike, the thought of the contempt she would feel for such behavior held him back.

"We'll leave it at that," she said. "I know you will help Mike if he ever needs it. And I hope you have a pleasant stay with the Penfolds. Remember what I've told you about attentions to your hostess, and don't forget to tip the servants. I must go up now and see that Cecily is settled. She always gets overexcited at times like this."

Rob stood up as she left the room. It was a customary thing. He stood afterward looking into the fire and listening to Mike's piano. What was customary and what was right. There was so much to get hold of, and then hang on to. It would never be easy and automatic for him as it was for those, like Mike, who had been born and reared to it. But he would get it right. He was determined about that.

Approaching it, the Penfolds' home looked more orderly and formal than Gifford House. It was smaller and more compact, built in the Georgian style and symmetrical in its features. Inside, though, there was a different contrast. There was a scarcely definable flavor of disorganization, of things being slightly out of place and wrong. The servants were slipshod and inefficient. On the first morning of their stay tea was brought late to the bedroom and was cold when it arrived. And Rob found that while an attempt had been made on his shoes he had to clean them properly himself.

Mr. Penfold, although physically quite unlike Mr. Gifford, being small and fat, also took a back seat in household affairs and also had a hobby which was something of an obsession. In his case it was clock-making. The house was filled with the products of his devotion—Rob found two in the room which he was given—and while they were there yet another was brought with pride from his workshop and prominently installed in the drawing room. It was an odd construction. The clock face surmounted the mast of a galleon which rocked steadily in a painted wooden sea. It made Rob a little queasy to look at it.

There was nothing at all in Mrs. Penfold that resembled Mrs. Gifford. Like her husband she was short and dumpy. She was also very plainly ineffectual. Her contribution to the domestic routine appeared to be one of going into mild panics whenever anything went wrong. Rob was sorry on her account the first time this happened, but he observed that the panic was of brief duration and soon forgotten. The rest of the time she talked almost incessantly in a fluttering voice without ever saying anything worth listening to.

Insofar as the house was organized at all, the Penfolds' daughter Lilian saw to it. She was in her thirties, unmarried, a woman with a long sallow face and deep close-set eyes under fierce brows. She had a sharp way of speaking and was usually either complaining or scolding—generally complaining about things the servants were doing wrong and scolding them for their mistakes. As far as could be seen this did not affect the situation in the slightest. Meals arrived late, lukewarm, and badly cooked. It was a far cry from the warmth and easy efficiency of Gifford House.

Daniel Penfold, by comparison with the others, seemed more pleasant on closer acquaintance. He had an unsureness, a modesty almost, which was disarming. It was possible, Rob thought, that his brother's presence had something to do with it. This was Roger, the ex-officer, who was in his late twenties. He seemed to share his sister's anger at life and the world, but in a sharper, more concentrated form. Daniel was obviously very much under his influence. Roger was the only member of the family who could have been called handsome. His features were clean cut but sharp, the gray eyes cold. When he was excited his mouth twitched a little at one corner.

This happened when Mike asked him some questions about China and the war. They were at dinner and he launched, disregarding his food, into a tirade on the subject. Tackling stringy boiled beef and lumpy potatoes with overdone cabbage, Rob felt he could sympathize with his lack of appetite but he did not make much of the argument. According to Roger Penfold the war could have been ended years, decades ago.

"It's a big country, isn't it?" Mike said. "I thought that as fast as one province gets quietened guerrilla fighters crop up in another."

"That's the story, but it won't wash. Nobody's trying to finish things. It's a useful place to pack people who might cause trouble if they stayed at home."

"You volunteered, though, didn't you?"

"Officers do. Some men. But most are drafted from the Conurb. They get the choice of China or long prison sentences. After seven years of military discipline, providing they've not been killed, they're glad enough to settle for an easy life."

He broke off to take a mouthful of food, but then laid knife and fork down again.

"The whole system is a conditioning and a conspiracy. Take money. We don't talk about it, do we? It's not the done thing. We have investments which we live on, but no one asks where they come from. Well, they come from the Conurbs. The Conurbans work in factories producing the goods and the gentry live on the profits. In the old days capitalists did at least have some contact with the source of their wealth, but that's all been eliminated. The money is washed and cleaned and passed across the Barrier with gloved hands."

For a moment Rob thought he was talking literally, and had a startling vision of coins being washed in some huge vat, carefully dried and then handed over the fence by a chain of gloved hands. He realized, though, that the remark was merely metaphorical. In any case money was different here—gold and silver instead of the flimsy paper and plastic tokens used in the Conurbs. Roger went on talking angrily about the wrongs of society. Mike was listening intently. Rob himself concentrated on trying to finish what was on his plate and hoped that the pudding would be a little better.

There was no opportunity for Rob and Mike to talk in private during the four days they spent with the Penfolds. But at last, to Rob's relief, the visit was over and they jogged together, on Captain and Sonnet, over open country in the direction of home. There had been a heavy frost and the air was still sharply cold, but the sun had risen in a blue and white sky.

"That butler . . ." Rob said. "I gave him half a sovereign as Aunt Margaret told me to, and he looked at it as though it were a sixpence. Do you think he's used to getting more than that?"

"I doubt it," Mike said. "He's just a naturally disgruntled type."

Rob could not resist saying, "I thought the atmosphere was a bit like that altogether."

"Dan's sister, you mean?"

"His brother too."

"There's a big difference. She's just on her way to becoming a sour old maid. He wants to do something, to change things and make them better."

"By that revolution you were talking about?"

"If necessary."

"Look, even supposing he *could* do it—could bust things up—what do you imagine he's going to be able to put in its place?"

"Something better."

"But *what?*"

"A society that could be free, could grow. Where people aren't conditioned into idleness or mass stupidity. Where someone like my father has more to exercise his mind than looking after comic little trees."

"Or Mr. Penfold with his clocks?"

"Exactly!"

"But that's being silly," Rob said. "There have always been people who had hobbies other people thought were ridiculous. And what would you expect them to do at their age, anyway?"

"It's not just them, though I think they're typical of

what's wrong. Everything's fallen back. What about space travel, for instance?"

Rob remembered the class in history of engineering and his query on exactly the same point. He gave the answer the master had given him: it had been of no possible benefit to mankind, fantastically wasteful of resources.

"What is of benefit to mankind?" Mike asked. "Three-day riding events? County cricket? Parties? Or holovision and the Games? And what's wasteful? Is there anything more wasteful than restricting human enterprise?"

"People are happy as they are," Rob insisted. "That's what matters." He saw Mike glance at him and added defensively, "The great majority anyway. And in any case I don't see the Penfolds organizing a revolution. They can't even organize their own home."

"That's Mrs. Penfold and Lilian. It's nothing to do with Roger."

"So Roger and Dan are going to do it on their own, are they?"

"There are others who look at things the same way. A lot."

There probably were a few, Rob thought. Half a dozen or a dozen, grousing over dinner tables, very likely because their digestions had been spoiled by bad cooking as the Penfolds' had been. Lots of talk with nothing coming of it but more talk. All the same . . . He remembered what Mrs. Gifford had said, about Roger's dubious reputation. It would do Mike no good to be associated with them. He began to say something of the sort, treading as warily as he could.

Mike listened for a time, and then said, "Mother's been on to you, hasn't she?"

"What do you mean?" Rob said awkwardly.

"She had a few words with me," Mike said, "after she read my last report. And I overheard a snatch here and there at Christmas while I was playing the piano and you were in the drawing room. There are some funny acoustics in that house."

"I didn't . . ."

"Tell her anything?" He grinned. "Don't worry. I know you wouldn't. And don't worry about me, either. She fusses at times."

There was nothing to worry about, really. This was just a craze of Mike's. People got them at times. Like the boy in the house who had spent the first half of term teaching himself to play the violin, and the second half whittling boats to launch in the stream that ran through the school grounds. The second enterprise had been as enthusiastic and pointless as the first, but less of a nuisance for everyone else.

"It's funny," Mike said.

"What is?"

"I don't suppose I would have been interested in any of this if I hadn't run across you that day."

Was that true, Rob wondered. It might be, in a way. But probably only because Mike had been bored and looking for something to get interested in. It was a pity it had to be something like this which could cause trouble. But if it were just a craze it would pass quickly enough. He went back to his satisfaction at having left the Penfolds. There was a long open stretch of hill ahead.

"Come on! Let's give them a gallop," he said to Mike.

The Lent term seemed to pass even quicker than the Michaelmas term had done. Rob felt he had settled into school by now and got the measure of things. It was not exactly a case of roses all the way—he had one bad spell in midterm with two beatings in three days—but he had to admit he was enjoying life. The high spot came with the junior cross-country run in which, after holding third place for most of the course, he managed a burst of speed which put him in front. His name, R. Perrott, would be added to the hundred others inscribed on the base of the big silver cup and in June, at Speech Day, he would be given the small silver replica to keep. He felt a twinge of pleasure when he thought of it.

End of term was one of a succession of cold wet days. The post coach, taking them home, flung up spray from puddles that had formed where the road surface was worn. It rained almost continuously for three days after that, and then the April sun dried and warmed the land. Spring budded and sparkled. The chestnuts were in delicate green leaf and soon would be in flower. Spelled chestnut for the tree, Rob reminded himself, but chesnut for the horse. One more thing which everyone in the County took for granted but which for him represented a conscious effort. But it was an effort that got easier all the time.

He rode with Mike into Oxford to buy presents for Cecily's birthday. From a distance they looked at the city, their horses reined in. Spires gleamed in the sunshine. Like Mike he would go there some day—to Christ Church which was where the Giffords had always gone. The House, as it was called, five hundred years old, brooded over by Tom Tower, having a cathedral inside its very walls for a chapel.

"Looks good," he said.

One did not enthuse about things that impressed one: it was not customary. Mike said, after a moment:

"Yes. Do you see over there?"

"Those fields?"

"There were factories there once. Making cars. Not elec-trocars. The old kind, with internal-combustion engines. It was one of the biggest in England. Perhaps the biggest."

The city was a jewel, the green fields a setting for it.

"Don't tell me you'd like to see them back?" Rob said.

They still argued about the state of society, but less frequently. They recognized that they were on opposite sides and that argument got them nowhere. There was a pause before Mike replied.

"No, I don't."

He moved forward on Captain and Rob on Sonnet followed suit. They rode into the city, tethered their horses at an inn just off the High, and did their shopping. Mike found a silk shawl for Cecily, bright red with a crimson fringe. Rob bought her a pendant, a small opal on a thin silver chain. It cost more than he could really afford, but he knew she would like it. After that they window-shopped for a time. Everything in the shops here looked so much more solid, more real, than the flashy trinkets and gadgets of the Conurb. There was a lot of silver and polished leather. He looked longingly at a magnificent bow with beautifully feathered arrows in a silver-banded quiver.

A clock chimed and he pulled out the pocket watch which had been his Christmas present from the Giffords, to check the time.

"Do you think we ought to be getting back for luncheon?"

"Look," Mike said, "you go on. I'll see you at the inn. I've remembered, there's a chap I've got to look up. About a horse."

"I'll come with you, if you like."

Mike shook his head. "No need. It won't take more than five minutes. I'd rather you ordered for me—they're usually a bit slow at that place. I'll have the steak pudding."

Rob had an impression there was more to it than that—that Mike did not want him with him. Well, that was his affair. He nodded, and walked away in the direction of the inn.

At the beginning of the holidays Mike and Rob had done some fly-fishing on the river running through the grounds of Gifford House. They caught quite a few trout, some of which they cooked and ate out of doors, picking the firm, slightly pink flesh off the bones with their fingers. Rob commented on the color and Mike told him they were called salmon trout though they had no connection with the salmon family. Their flesh was pink because they fed largely on a tiny pink shrimp.

He had suggested they should go salmon fishing some time. In the last twenty years these had been coming up to the higher reaches of the Thames, and the Giffords had friends with a stretch of the river who had given the family a permanent invitation to fish it. They were the Beechings whom Rob had met a couple of times already. He was a huge, corpulent man, she a small, thin woman. They had no children of their own but liked the company of young people.

After their visit to Oxford, Mike made a definite arrangement for the pair of them to ride over the following Friday. Then, on the Thursday, he himself backed out. It was the business of the horse again. His father had given him permission to look for another hunter and this coper in Oxford claimed he had the chance of a very good one. The opportunity of seeing it had come up earlier than he had expected, and he would have to take it. The man claimed other parties were interested.

"That's all right," Rob said. "We can put the salmon fishing off. We've time enough before we go back."

"I'd rather you didn't. The Beechings are expecting us for luncheon. I thought you could make apologies for me. They'll be very disappointed if we both drop out."

"If you think so," Rob said. "I hope you get the horse."

"So do I. Harry will have to look at it as well, of course."

"Are you taking him with you?"

"No."

"Wouldn't it be more sensible?"

"I don't think so." He sounded slightly irritated. "Mr. Lavernham would have to examine him as well before we bought him." Mr. Lavernham was the vet. "I want to see him myself in the first place."

It seemed a cumbersome way of doing things, but presumably Mike knew what he was about.

"Fair enough. You'd better give me directions for getting to the Beechings'. Let's go and look at a map."

It was some distance from Gifford House, on the far side of a low ridge of hills. The sun was well up by the time Rob came to the river. He could see the Beechings' house across the meadows, recognizable by a cone-topped tower nearby which Mike told him had been built by some eccentric ancestor: there were lots of follies of this kind scattered about the County. The arrangement had been to fish through the morning and only after that call on the Beechings. He tethered Sonnet where she could crop comfortably and took up his position on the river bank.

For some time he had no luck. The salmon were there —he saw their long sinuous bodies, scales gleaming, rise to take flies—but they ignored his lure. It was a couple of hours before he got a bite. The fish fought hard and eventually broke loose. There was another long and discouraging blank period. Then, inside half an hour, he landed three, two of four or five pounds, the third an eight-pounder at least. The day was hot by now. He wiped sweat from his face and hands and decided it was time to call a halt. He was to be at the house before one, and it was after twelve.

He rode across the meadows in a glow of satisfaction. He would have something to show Mike when he got back. He was thinking about this when he saw a troop of horsemen galloping along the road, a field away. It was a sight which no longer caused apprehension, but he was curious. The patrols were made up of young men who liked the exercise and display, and the rivalry between troops which was chiefly shown in point-to-point races and riding events.

They went out in the morning and evening, not in the middle of the day. And this was too big—much too big. Instead of half a dozen there was a score of riders. More, even. He watched them disappear along the road to Oxford and turned Sonnet toward the house.

He found confusion there, with servants dashing about in different directions. He called to one and got an unintelligible reply. He dismounted and was looking for a groom to take his horse when he saw Mrs. Beeching coming toward him from the house. She looked very white. Rob made a small bow of greeting, and asked, "Is there something wrong? Can I help?"

"Have you not heard the news?"

He shook his head. "I've been on the river."

"A terrible thing." Her voice trembled. "Terrible. Who would believe it could happen?"

"What's happened, ma'am?" he said urgently.

"A rebellion. But why? How? It's unbelievable. They've taken Oxford. And Bristol . . ."

Oxford, he thought. Mike. The man with the horse had been his excuse to get away. He must be in it. But it was all incredible. Violence was something that happened in China, or in the mindless drunken riots of the Conurbs. It could not happen here, in the peace and security of the County. And Bristol was the County's capital, headquarters of the government.

"They can't have taken Bristol. How could they?"

"They used guns."

There was a world of shock and horror in her voice. Guns had been controlled out of existence for so long that the controls themselves had been forgotten. They were used in the war, half a world away, but not here in England. Not even in the Conurbs, where knives and blackjacks were the limit of the criminal's armory. It was almost impossible to accept, yet he knew what she said must be true. Nothing else could explain the capture of the cities. Roger Penfold, he thought, and others like him . . . they must have smuggled guns back from the East somehow.

"I saw a troop of horsemen on the road," he said.

"The vigilantes are forming," Mrs. Beeching said. "But it may be too late. My husband has gone with them. He's too old and . . . not strong enough. But he would go."

Another time the thought of fat old Mr. Beeching riding into battle would have been laughable, but Rob did not feel like laughing. "I must get back,"

"Have something to eat first."

Rob shook his head. "I'd better go."

Gifford House had a deserted look. The stables were empty except for a horse that had gone lame a few days before. There was no groom to take Sonnet so Rob had to see to her himself. He was rubbing her down when he heard a sound and turned to see Mrs. Gifford.

"Have they all . . . ?" he asked.

"Gone with the vigilantes. Your uncle, too."

"Do you know where they're gathering, Aunt Margaret? I'll go after them."

"No. You're too young."

"I can use a sword. I got a good report for swordplay and fencing. I want to do something."

"They don't need the help of boys," she said. "At least, our side does not. Where is Mike, Rob?"

"I don't know. He said . . ."

"I want the truth from you." There was cold anger in her voice. "I think I'm entitled to that. He's mixed up in this, isn't he?"

"I don't know." Her look cut him like a knife. "I think so."

"Tell me what you know. Everything."

There was no point, he told himself, in keeping the confidence any longer. Even if there had been, he doubted if he could have resisted her demand. He feared her anger, wanted her not to hate him. He spoke of the meeting in Penfold's study and of the things that had happened afterward.

When he had finished she said, "I told you at Christmas I was worried about Mike, and asked your help. Was this the best you could do? Wash your hands of the whole thing?"

"I argued with him."

"Argued!"

"He only spoke of revolt at the beginning. I thought it was just a wild idea, that it couldn't come to anything. The whole thing seemed crazy."

She stared at him. "You were a runaway when Mike found you. A Conurban. Hungry and thirsty, dirty, frightened, in rags and a scarecrow's coat. He helped you, looked after you, persuaded us to take you in, to make you one of the family. I hope you are happy over the way you have repaid him."

She turned and walked out of the stable. Rob felt sick. Mechanically he went on seeing to the horse. If he could make his way to where the fighting was he might find Mike, perhaps help him. After that . . . Whatever happened he could not come back here. He supposed he would have to think about that some time but at the moment it did not matter.

He resaddled Sonnet and led her out. He had mounted and was riding toward the drive when his name was called. Mrs. Gifford stood by the back door. She called again and he went to her.

"Where are you going?"

"Away, ma'am."

She put her hand on the rein. "I spoke too harshly to you. What's done is done."

Rob shook his head. "I've got to go."

"The men have all gone," she said. "Cecily and I are alone except for the maids. Stay with us, Rob."

Her eyes held his. Her face was strained and old, but beautiful. He realized that she needed him, that this was a different acceptance from the other. He nodded and dismounted.

9

A Visitor at Night

The day passed slowly. The telephone exchange was not operating and they had no clear idea what was happening. A peddler with his packhorse came by and filled the heads of the maids with rumors and alarms. There had been massacres. At Oxford the Cherwell had run red with blood. Hordes of Conurbans had smashed a way through the Barrier and were killing and destroying and burning everything in their path. All lies, probably—peddlers' stories were notorious—but one could not be certain. Before going to bed Rob checked that all the doors were locked and bolted. A murderous mob would presumably break in through the windows, anyway, but it was something to do.

He went past Cecily's bedroom to reach his own. She called him in.

"Are you all right?" Rob asked.

She was sitting up in bed. "I heard footsteps," she said, "and I was frightened. Then I realized it was you."

"There was nothing to be frightened of."

"Why hasn't Mike come back?"

"He's staying with friends until the trouble's over."

"When will that be?"

"Soon."

"You're sure?"

"Quite sure."

The lumoglobe was not lit. There was only the flicker of the night light on the table beside her bed. The room was full of shadows.

"Kiss me goodnight?" she said.

He kissed her forehead and she snuggled down. As he went toward the door she said, "Rob?"

"Yes?"

"I'm glad you're here."

"Go to sleep. It will soon be morning."

He went to his own room and stood for a long time staring out into the darkness before he got into bed.

The morning was somber with rain falling steadily from a sodden gray sky. Mrs. Gifford tried the telephone again but with no success. Rob suggested riding out to see if any of the neighboring houses had reliable news but she opposed the idea and he did not persist. The hours dragged by and for the first time Rob found himself missing the know-it-all reportage of the holovision newscasters. He went to the conservatory to water Mr. Gifford's miniature trees. Rain still dripped heavily on the glass. He heard Cecily's

voice and then her hurrying footsteps. She was in the doorway, excited and afraid.

"What is it?" he said.

"Horsemen." Her breast was heaving. "Mummy saw
them from the drawing room. Coming up from the wood."

He asked no more questions but ran, Cecily running with
him. Mrs. Gifford turned from the window.

"Your eyes are better than mine." she said.

There were half a dozen. He recognized Harry the groom
first on a big bay horse called Miller, then Mr. Gifford.

"It's all right, Aunt Margaret. It's them."

They went out into the rain and were soaking wet by the
time the horsemen reached them. Mrs. Gifford looked up
at her husband.

"What's happened?"

"Haven't you been told?"

"There's no telephone. Are they fighting still?"

He shook his head. "It's all over."

"And?"

"It's been put down. We weren't needed. Everything is
under control. My dear, you're drenched through. Go back
inside. I'll come as soon as we've got the horses in."

She did not move. "Mike?"

"I don't know." he said heavily. "I heard young Penfold
was killed but it was only a rumor. Nothing about Mike."

The rain stopped for a couple of hours in the afternoon
and then came on more remorselessly than ever. The telephone was working again by teatime and Mrs. Gifford
called several people but could get no news of Mike. His

name was not on the provisional list of dead and wounded but it was known to be incomplete. The authorities were occupied with getting things tidied up. No list of prisoners had been issued yet.

What was certain was that the revolt had been crushed: nothing remained in the hands of the rebels. Details were vague, but it seemed that the government had kept a reserve of weapons. Guns had been answered by guns. The only way the revolt could have succeeded would have been through popular support and this had been nonexistent. There had been attempts to win over the servant class as a body but they had failed miserably. The story of an invasion from the Conurbs was entirely false. The whole affair, alarming as it might have seemed, had merely demonstrated the strength and stability of the system.

This was small comfort for the Giffords. After dinner Mr. Gifford sat by himself with the heavy silver-topped port decanter in front of him on the walnut table. Coming to say goodnight to him, Rob saw that his hands were shaking.

"As long as he's alive . . ." Mr. Gifford said. "They won't be too hard on him. He's only a boy."

There was silence except for the ticking of the old wall clock, whose face also showed the phases of the moon, and a man and woman on a seesaw who predicted the weather. The little man had risen higher than his partner, promising a better day tomorrow. Mr. Gifford poured himself another glass of port.

"I mustn't keep you up, Rob. You need your sleep. Goodnight, my boy."

Rob was very tired—he had not slept well the previous

night—but sleep would not come. He lay in bed staring out at a night that now was silvered with moonlight. The clouds were rolling away at the little man's bidding.

The tap on the door startled him. Cecily, he thought, wanting company. "Come in."

The door opened. There was no light on the landing and the moonlight did not extend that far. The figure was vague, but it was not Cecily. He started to speak but was interrupted.

"It's me."

Mike came in and quietly closed the door behind him.

Rob got out of bed. "We must keep quiet," Mike whispered. "Father's still up."

"I know. How did you get in?"

"Through the kitchen. Cook leaves a window open for the cats."

He was shivering. His clothes were wet, his hair plastered across his forehead. Keeping his own voice down, Rob said, "Better get those things off. I'll bring some dry clothes and a towel for you to rub down."

He got them from Mike's room and Mike dried himself and changed. Rob asked him why he had not gone to his own room first.

"You might have heard me moving about and raised an alarm without thinking. And I wasn't sure they wouldn't have someone in there waiting for me."

The first point seemed reasonable, the second absurd. Having been part of a conspiracy Mike saw tricks and stratagems everywhere.

"Was it difficult getting back?"

"I had to lie up until dark. Luckily Captain has eyes better than most cats."

"Where is he?"

"Captain? Tied up by the shrubbery. I didn't dare take him to the stables in case he woke one of the grooms. But I got in myself and got a blanket for him, and oats."

"What about you? When did you eat last?"

"A meal? Yesterday. But I'm all right. I wolfed a cold chicken from the larder."

"Look," Rob said, "don't you think you ought to tell your people you're here? They've been worried sick about you."

"I know. I'm sorry. But I don't want to involve them."

"They're involved already."

Mike did not answer. His face in the moonlight was tired and drawn. He looked as though he had been through it.

"What happened?" Rob said.

"We lost. You heard, I suppose."

"Yes."

"They had guns as well."

"You used them first, though," Rob said.

"And copters? And gas bombs?"

"I didn't hear about that."

"They were what finished us. They let us take over. Then when we were concentrated, they came down with copters dropping nerve gas. It paralyzes on a medium dose, kills on a severe one. I was lucky. I was on the fringe. The whiff I got only made me sick."

"You couldn't expect them to stand by and let you win. It was probably the quickest way, and the least bloody."

"And caused very little damage to private property, another important point. They were waiting for us. This peaceful elegant society with its horses and ornamental swords and code of good manners . . . behind it there's force, advanced weapons, ruthlessness."

"Is that so terrible? Surely you must expect people to defend themselves?"

"You don't see it." Mike spoke with a cold flat anger. "It's all a fake, a show for puppets. Do as you're told in that station to which it has pleased God to call you and you're all right. Step out of line and you get smashed."

"You were all gentry, weren't you? The servants didn't support the rebellion."

"No, they didn't support us. That's a point for the government, isn't it? It shows this was just the work of a few bored and dissatisfied people—that everything's splendid otherwise. The servants have been better conditioned: that's all. They've been taught to want what they've got."

"Perhaps what they've got isn't so bad, compared with what might be. With revolutions in the past there were things to fight against—hunger, oppression, slavery. The servants are well cared for. They look up to the gentry and have the Conurbans to look down on. Why should they want a change?"

"No, why should they?" Mike asked wearily.

"People are happy enough, both here and in the Conurb. What's the *point* in trying to turn things upside down?"

"The same old argument." He gave Rob a lopsided grin. "We don't see things the same way, do we? Lord, I'm tired."

"Go to bed. Get some rest."

Mike shook his head. "It's a risk being here at all. It's the place where they're bound to look for me."

"It will be days before they sort the mess out. Weeks more likely."

"Don't be fooled by the apparent confusion. We were. The society we live in is more organized than it seems."

"Let me tell your parents you're here. Your mother, anyway. She could help you."

Mike yawned. "Out of the question."

"What do you think you're going to do?"

"I'll manage."

"But it's finished. You admit that. You'll have to give yourself up sooner or later. They won't do anything to you. They probably won't do much to any of the rebels since it's been crushed so easily. I suppose you may get expelled from school."

"Expelled?" Mike laughed. "I hadn't thought of that."

"But you agree you'll have to surrender eventually. You can't hide out forever."

"Don't I recall saying something like that to you once upon a time?" Mike said whimsically. "We've made quite a switch, haven't we? You here, me on the run. Funny when you think about it."

"Well, what you said was true. You would be on your own, as I was. Your friends are all prisoners."

"Or dead. Not quite all, though. Some escaped. The most important one did."

"And everyone in the County will be hunting for you."

"In the County, yes."

His tone was enigmatic.

"What does that mean?" Rob asked.

"The important one—he made preparations in case of failure. He reckoned it would be impossible to do anything in the County. But we have friends in the Conurbs."

"There was no rising there. It was just a rumor."

"No rising was intended. Not at this time, anyway. If we had controlled the County it wouldn't have been necessary. It doesn't mean there isn't an opposition in the Conurbs, that we can't work from there. It will take longer, that's all."

"Are you saying this is going to go on, that you still hope for a revolution?"

"Yes, of course."

"You're crazy. Even if there were any sense in it, it's impossible. You can't hope to win. You must know that by now."

"No good saying we can't hope, because we do." Mike shrugged. "Our chances may not be very bright, but they're better than no chance at all and no hope."

"You mean you're intending to go . . ."

"Over the Barrier. A reverse journey from yours."

"And live there—in the Conurb?" Rob said incredulously.

"Yes."

"In crowds and noise and squalor? You'd hate every minute of it. I know what it's like. You don't. Plotting in country houses and taking part in a revolt for a few hours isn't the same as living as a Conurban, day after day, month after month."

"I didn't imagine I was going to enjoy it."

He was serious, Rob saw. He was torn by conflicting feelings. He felt he was letting Mike down again—that Mrs. Gifford's jibe about repaying help was still true. On the other hand . . .

"You're wrong about this," he said. "I'm sure you'll come around to seeing it. When you do, even if you are in the Conurb, you can come back. If I went . . ."

"It would be a different proposition. I know." He put a hand on Rob's shoulder. "If you wanted to come I wouldn't take you."

"Don't go," Rob said. "Nothing will happen to you if you surrender to the police."

Mike looked at him. "You think not?"

"I'm sure. Now there's no danger . . ."

"Leave it," Mike said. "I've made up my mind."

"If you would just talk to your parents—let them know that you're here, that you're safe."

"If I did, do you think they would let me go again?" Rob was silent. Mike went on, "I suppose I ought not to have come back, but it was on my way and I thought I had a better chance of stealing food here than anywhere else. At another place a dog might have barked. Tess only tried to lick me all over. I mustn't hang about, though. I want to get across the fence by morning. The moonlight's a help."

"And Captain? You can't very well take him with you."

"No." He managed a smile, a small one. "I'll turn him loose. He'll find his way home."

"Change your mind!" Rob said. "You still can."

"No."

"I could raise the alarm—call your father."

"But you won't."

He said it with conviction and Rob knew it was true. He pointed to the pile of wet and dirty clothing.

"I'll ditch those in the morning."

"Thanks. I'm off now. If you should change *your* mind about the way things are . . ." He smiled. "Unlikely, I know. But just in case, I'm heading for the Southampton Conurb. A place called Eastleigh. Desborough Road, number two-four-four. You'll find me there, or someone who can tell you where I am."

"I'll see you off."

"No. Better not."

"On the contrary. If we do disturb anyone I can do the answering. Say I felt restless and went wandering. To the kitchen, perhaps, because I was hungry. It accounts for that chicken."

"A good point. Let's go then."

The stairs creaked but they did not disturb anyone. The lamplight under the door of the drawing room showed that Mr. Gifford was still up with his port but they crept past quietly and unobserved. In the kitchen Mike took a loaf and several thick slices off a leg of ham.

They climbed in turn through the window. The moonlight shone on the bank of retreating cloud, low in the west, outlining the house and the shapes of trees. Captain whinnied softly as Mike approached him.

They shook hands and said good-by. Wasting no more time, Mike mounted and rode off across the black and silver grass.

10

The Guardians

They looked like an ordinary patrol. They wore scarlet tunics and high leather boots and swords swung from their belts. The leader also looked ordinary but unthinkably he had entered the house without being announced or even waiting for leave. He found the family at breakfast. He was a lean, dark man in his late twenties with a thin nose that had been broken and badly set at some time and a mouth that was almost smiling but not quite. He made a quick bow, clicking his heels.

"I hope you will forgive the lack of ceremony." He spoke rapidly in a dry tone that did not indicate much interest whether he was forgiven or not. "This is urgent, government business. My name is Marshall. Captain Marshall."

Rob noticed something unusual—in fact extraordinary.

On the other side of his belt there was a leather holster, protruding from it the butt of a pistol.

"Is it—to do with my son?" Mr. Gifford said.

"What about your son?"

"I thought . . ."

The eyes were cold, the skin around them wrinkled and leathery as though from long staring into harsh sunlight and bleak winds. Compared with the normal gentleman of the County he looked both wilder and more disciplined. A veteran, Rob guessed, of the China War.

"Have you seen your son since the rebellion?"

Mr. Gifford shook his head. Mrs. Gifford asked in a strained voice, "Do you have any news of him, Captain?"

"Only, ma'am, that his name is on the list of those against whom warrants have been issued for arrest on a charge of armed rebellion."

"Then he's alive!"

"He may be. I have no information to the contrary." His gaze went to Mr. Gifford. "You understand that if your son returns home the authorities must be informed and he must be held until a patrol arrives to take him into custody?"

"Yes," Mr. Gifford said, "I understand that."

"They won't put him in prison?" Cecily burst out.

Ignoring her, Marshall continued, "If you do have information as to his whereabouts you will please disclose it to me."

"I have no information," Mr. Gifford said wearily.

Marshall stared for a moment in silence, then said, "And if any such intelligence comes to you in the future you will notify the appropriate authorities. Is that also understood? The penalty for failure could be heavy."

"Yes," Mr. Gifford said, "it is understood. If you have now fulfilled the purpose of your mission, Captain, we will not keep you from your duties."

Marshall gave a small shake of the head. "That is not the purpose of my mission." He looked at Rob, sharply appraising. "This is Rob Perrott, I believe, a distant relation of Mrs. Gifford, who lives with you."

"Yes," Mr. Gifford said. "The son of my wife's cousin."

A slight nod, the eyes still watching. Marshall said:

"My instructions are that he is to accompany me for questioning."

Mr. Gifford was silent.

"He is not involved in any way," Mrs. Gifford said. "Our son is—we accept that. But not Rob. You have our word on it."

Marshall's eyebrows lifted slightly but otherwise his expression did not change. "Those are my instructions." He paused, and added, "The boys lived together and were at school together. Something may have been said, some hint given, which could be useful. Possibly the boy himself does not appreciate this. This is not an arrest and he will be well looked after."

"Where are you taking him?" Mrs. Gifford asked.

Marshall did not answer that, but repeated, "He will be well looked after."

"And how long will you keep him?"

"Not long. No longer than is necessary."

Rob rode at Marshall's side with the rest of the patrol clattering behind them. Marshall spoke little and his manner did not encourage Rob to talk. It was not until they swung down a familiar road and he saw park gates in the distance that he said, "Are we going to Old Hall, then?"

Marshall glanced at him. "Yes."

He was greatly relieved. The disciplined silence of Marshall and his patrol and the guns, had conjured up a picture of a gloomy prisonlike building somewhere, in Bristol perhaps, and harsh inquisitors. To be taken to Sir Percy Gregory's home, where he had won his medal for archery, was far less alarming. Hopes continued to rise when he was handed over not to any military figure but to Sir Percy's butler, Jenks, a man of impressive but not unkindly appearance, who remembered him and spoke with courteous amiability.

He waited in a long oak-paneled hall. The walls were lined with oil paintings of past Gregorys, more than a score of them, interspersed with the heads of stags. One, between two men in ruffles and lace with long wigs, had enormous antlers: he counted twenty-three points. Typically County, and reassuring.

The butler, returning, said, "Sir Percy will see you in his study, Master Rob. If you will follow me."

There was a very large desk, its top covered with shiny green leather, by one of the windows, but Sir Percy was not sitting behind it. As Rob entered he was at the sideboard pouring a glass of whiskey from a decanter.

"Ah, there you are, my boy! I should think you'd like a little refreshment, eh? Lemonade, or coffee?"

"I would like coffee, sir."

"See to that, Jenks. And some cake or a few biscuits. We're not lunching for a couple of hours. Now, Rob, come and make yourself comfortable."

Rob's spirits rose higher still. There did not seem much to be alarmed about if he were invited to luncheon. Two wide low leather armchairs stood on either side of the hearth where a fire was burning brightly. Sir Percy settled Rob in one and took the other himself.

"Late in the year for a fire but I like the look of it. And there's a nip in the air still. Touch of frost early this morning. Now then, I imagine you'll have some idea of what I want to have a chat with you about."

His squatness filled the width of the armchair in whose twin Rob felt lost. But there was nothing threatening about his bulk, nor about the moustache, black flecked with white, curling above the thick lips and the chin with the deep cleft in it. He looked like a friendly uncle. Friendly and not particularly intelligent, but one would still need to be wary.

"About Mike, sir?"

"Yes." Sir Percy shook his head. "A sad little to-do, this. I've known him all his life, of course. There's a distant connection on the male side. The boy needs help."

Rob half nodded but did not say anything. Sir Percy repeated, "He needs help from all of us. Tell me, did he talk to you about this business?"

"No, sir."

"That's a bit strange, isn't it? You're his cousin. You live with him, you're both in College House."

There was no threat in the tone.

"We did not see all that much of each other at school. We're in different forms. We have different friends, too."

"Yes. Still, I should have thought he might have said something to you."

The eyes blinked at him shrewdly.

"He was probably fairly sure I wouldn't be on their side," Rob said. "And if so it would be taking an unnecessary risk to tell me anything."

"That's a good point," Sir Percy conceded. "Ah, here's nourishment. Put the tray down on the little table, Jenks. You can help yourself, Rob."

There was steaming coffee in one silver pot, hot milk in the other. Rob poured himself a cup and took a slice of cherry cake. Sir Percy said, "Tuck in. I like to see a lad with an appetite. You were raised in Nepal, weren't you? And your mother is . . ."

"She and Aunt Margaret are cousins."

"That's right. And your father . . ."

Rob filled in the details, volunteering information before it was requested. He had the background and story pat by now. After all, on the day of the garden party he had fooled Sir Percy's friend, who had lived in the country. He knew he was telling it well.

Sir Percy finished his whiskey and went to pour another.

"You're a bright boy, Rob." He had his back to him, getting the drink. But there was, Rob had already noticed, a mirror in the sideboard which had him in view. He gave a slightly embarrassed smile.

Sir Percy turned around, glass in hand.

"Yes," he said. "You're a bright boy, Rob Randall."

The sound of his own name shocked him into rigidity. Sir Percy's broad face still wore an expression of slightly stupid amiability but that was now the reverse of reassuring. He realized he had been cunningly led into exposing himself as a skilled liar.

Sir Percy did not return to his armchair but went around the desk and seated himself in a heavy high-backed chair. He took a file out of a drawer. Opening it, he read:

"Robin Randall, born August 17th, 2038, in the Fulham sector of Greater London. Father, John Randall, born Basingstoke 1998, died Charing Cross Hospital, April 2052: heart failure following electric shock. Mother, Jennifer Hilda Randall, maiden name Gallagher, born 2007, died 2049: carcinoma. Birthplace: Shearham, Gloucestershire."

He looked up. "Is that what gave you the idea of crossing over?"

They knew everything about him. Denial would be absurd. He said in a low voice, "Partly, sir."

"Yes." Sir Percy nodded. "Did your mother ever talk about the County?"

"No. I didn't know she came from here until . . . I found some letters after my father died."

"An interesting point," Sir Percy said. "Would the discovery in itself be enough to allow an enterprising youngster to break the conditioned taboos against the County, or did she, even without saying anything, unconsciously predispose you in that direction? Worth bringing up at the next meeting of the Psychosocial Committee. Still, that's not immediately to the point. Do you have anything to say for yourself?"

"How long have you known about me?"

He realized as he spoke that it was not up to him to put the questions. Sir Percy did not seem to mind.

"Since three days after you went to live with the Giffords. That was, of course, some time before you gave that very convincing show for the benefit of Charlie Harcourt. Typical Nepalese settler twang!" He smiled. "A pity I can't put him in the picture. It would be amusing to see his face."

He closed the file and settled back in his chair.

"You can, of course, no longer be treated as an ordinary member of our society. You are not one, after all. You are a Conurban, posing as County. You are listed by the Conurb police as a runaway from the boarding school at Barnes. So I don't mind telling you that this society is not so haphazard and unorganized as it seems. Things are investigated and checked: thoroughly. We had the boy from Nepal and the absentee from the boarding school matched within twenty-four hours of the first automatic query.

"And now I will put a question to you. Since we know who you are and know that you were befriended by Michael Gifford, who persuaded his family to take you into their home, do you think it would be reasonable for me to believe that he never said anything to you about this plot?"

Rob shook his head. "No, sir."

"I'm glad you are being sensible. Now tell me everything. Take your time."

Rob told him, leaving out only Mike's visit during the night. Sir Percy listened without interruption. At the end, he said, "But he never spoke to you of the actual plans for the revolt? Isn't that a little improbable?"

"Not really, sir. I'd refused to go in with him."

"Why did you refuse?"

"I saw nothing wrong with things as they are. I mean, I . . ."

"You had succeeded in crossing over and had found a niche in the County and were satisfied with that. Do I have it right?"

"Yes, sir."

"But he might have hoped to win you to his views?"

"We had arguments, very fierce at times. We could never agree."

"You knew that what he was proposing amounted to treason?"

"I didn't think anything would happen. I thought it was all talk."

"Treasonable talk, though?" Sir Percy paused. "Why did you not report it to the authorities—to your tutor at school, at least?"

"Mike had helped me, sir."

"Yes." Sir Percy looked at him speculatively. "And if you *had* gone to the authorities you would almost certainly have been exposed as an imposter."

Rob was silent. He wanted to protest against the cynical motivation Sir Percy was attributing to him, but realized there would be no point in doing so.

After a moment, Sir Percy said, "You've not been much help to us, have you? You've told us nothing we didn't know already. Young Penhold's dead and we've got his brother."

Rob did not say anything. Sir Percy went on, "So I suppose the only thing to do is to pack you back to the place at Barnes."

It had been inevitable from the moment he was called by his true name. He tried to tell himself it might have been worse, a lot worse. He realized Sir Percy was talking again.

". . . society as we know it. For the first time in human history we have peace, plenty, the greatest happiness for the greatest number. Such violence and aggression as is unavoidable because inherent in man's nature is carefully channeled: in the Conurbs into Games-watching and occasional riots, in the County into athletic contests, hunting and so on. For cases where these things do not provide sufficient release we have the China War.

"In the Conurbs the masses are better fed and cared for—more contented—than they have ever been. In the County we have a leisured class who can enjoy a truly aristocratic way of life. We have stopped the clock, taken it back even, to the time before the First World War. It is a Golden Age which has lasted half a century and which need never end."

Sir Percy got up and walked over to one of the windows. The sun was shining; his carefully groomed hair and moustache gleamed in a ray of light. Rob wondered why he was telling him all this—if in fact he was just talking for his own satisfaction. He continued:

"It must *appear* natural because people cannot be contented unless they believe their lives to be natural. But to do this and to keep everything in balance requires intelligence and planning. It requires a special group of dedicated men who will act as guardians over the rest. Thus guns are abolished but a reserve is kept to protect society against insurrection. Not only that—we have psychologists to help us mold people into proper courses of action. We are constantly on the alert for trouble. The Conurb is easier to control than the County in that respect. Anyone showing creative intelligence and initiative stands out conspicuously from the mob and can be dealt with. Here it is less easy. Aristocracies have always provided the seedbeds for revolt. However well we manipulate the gentry, sooner or later there must be an eruption. This is what we have just had. We have watched it gather like a boil and at the right moment have lanced it. It will be fifty years at least before it happens again."

Sir Percy broke off. "Do you understand me, boy? I am not talking over your head?"

"No, sir."

"I did not think I was. You are intelligent, and that you have initiative was shown by your coming over to the County. The taboo against that has been carefully built up by our psychological experts and no ordinary boy would break it. Would you like to stay here instead of being sent back to the Conurb?"

He could not believe he was really being offered this. He said warily,

"Can I, sir? I thought . . ."

"You have been under observation since we discovered you, as a potential recruit to the guardians. Young Gifford was also considered at one time." He shrugged. "We make mistakes occasionally, but they can always be adjusted."

"But I'm a Conurban . . ."

"And not the first. You must learn to think behind these labels even though you continue to live with them. You will return as Rob Perrott and lead a normal life, with the Giffords and at school, later at university. You will seem to be an ordinary member of the gentry. In fact you will be one of those who govern behind the scenes. You may or may not have an official position in due course but if you do it will be, like mine, no more than a blind. The real power you exercise will be different and much greater."

He felt dazed. It was difficult to take in the change in his circumstances.

"Will you accept?"

He nodded. "Yes, sir."

Sir Percy smiled. "I thought you would. I like the look of you, Rob—have done from the beginning." He offered his hand and Rob took it. His grip was firm. "There's just one thing before we put all this on one side and start thinking about luncheon. You like venison, I hope? The thing is, we've jumped the gun in approaching you and for a particular reason. Normally you would not have been tackled for a few years. But we have this present business to tidy up. In particular, we have one or two people to find. Young Gifford is one, though not an important one. But he can lead us to the others. We think there is a good chance he might get in touch with you. He helped you, and he might look for help in return. Give it to him by all means but keep me informed. Before you leave I'll give you a two-way radio." He smiled again. "It's small but I don't need to tell you to keep it well hidden. Radio is something else that's not customary in the County."

"If you find Mike . . ." Rob said.

"We hope we'll also find bigger fish."

"But Mike himself . . ."

"You're worried about what happens to him? That's understandable. We guardians are not limited by the moralities we lay down for others but I hope we retain human feelings. He will be all right. You have my word for that. A very small operation on the brain, performed by expert surgeons. It won't hurt him. He'll remain active, intelligent, capable of a full life. But he won't want to rebel any more. It's a tried and tested technique. We keep it in reserve for cases like this."

He put an arm around Rob's shoulder. "And now let's talk about something else. How's your archery coming along?"

One of the maids made up the fire and with a little bob to Mrs. Gifford withdrew. The long velvet curtains were drawn against the night and the lamps cast soft radiant glows. One on the table beside Mrs. Gifford lit up the curve of her cheek, a few strands of gray in the brown of her hair, the tapestry on which she was working—a country scene with nymphs and shepherds. Cecily had gone to bed. Mr. Gifford now stirred restlessly in his armchair and got up.

"Think I'll go and have a look at the trees," he said. "Haven't had a chance to see to them today."

He picked up a lamp and took it with him. In the Conurb he could have switched on lumoglobes to light his way. Carrying a lamp was more trouble, as many things in this life were. But people had the time to take trouble and were happier for doing so. Rob thought of the servants, who had refused to join the rebellion. Perhaps they had been conditioned to like their present life, but that did not alter the fact of their liking it. Just as Mr. Gifford would rather carry a lamp to the conservatory than walk down a corridor lit with lumoglobes.

Rob had told the Giffords only that he had been questioned by Sir Percy, that Sir Percy had been satisfied that he knew nothing, and that he had lunched with him before being sent back. They had accepted this, more concerned with their anxiety over Mike. Mr. Gifford could not settle to anything. Mrs. Gifford worked in silence on her embroidery. Even Cecily was quiet and unhappy.

Rob himself was still confused by what had happened. He put down his book and looked around the room—the furniture with a patina of centuries, the china in its cabinet, so carefully dusted by one of the maids every week, the gleam of polished silver and the soft warm colors of Persian carpets. This was Mike's by right, not his. He was an interloper, a cuckoo in the nest. But Mike had rejected it, and no one could do anything about that. He had done his best to stop him. He could have done no more. It would have been stupid to cut himself off from it all simply because Mike had done so.

Something was different tonight. It was not just Mike being absent but something else, something more positive. He realized with a little shock what it was: for the first time he was really safe. Safe in the protection not merely of the Giffords but of something more powerful. The radio was carefully hidden. At the press of a button he could be in touch with the duty office in Oxford, with the whole secret organization of the guardians.

A log slipped in the fire and he took the tongs and set it right. Mrs. Gifford looked up and thanked him. As he went back to his chair, she said, "Tell me something."

"Yes, Aunt Margaret?"

"What did Mike say to you?"

She was watching him.

"When?"

"Last night."

He wondered if it were a guess, or if she knew something. While he hesitated, she went on:

"I told you once before that food missing from a kitchen is likely to be noticed."

"I'm afraid I got hungry in the night. I'm sorry I . . ."

"Very hungry, indeed. A whole cold roast chicken, a loaf of bread, part of a ham. But that was only the starting point. If Mike had been here he would probably have needed dry clothes. I checked his drawers and found several things missing."

She looked at him steadily. "It was a guess that you had seen him. I knew he had been here, but he might just have taken things and gone. But if you say you were hungry in the night . . . what happened, Rob?"

He told her that Mike had come, talked for a while, and left: nothing about his plan to go into the Conurb.

"Why didn't you stop him going?"

"I couldn't. I argued with him but he wouldn't listen. I asked him at least to talk to you and Uncle Joe but he wouldn't. He said if he did you wouldn't let him go."

"You did, though."

"I had no choice."

"You say his father was still up? Could you not have called him?"

"He trusted me not to. How could I, Aunt Margaret?"

She was staring at him. He looked for the cold anger she had shown on the day of the rebellion but it was not there. Instead her face showed a terrible sadness and desolation which was worse.

"You knew what had happened and what would happen —that he was being hunted. And yet you let him go without telling us he was here."

"If I had," he cried, "you would have given him up! He said that. And you would, wouldn't you?"

"Yes. He is only a boy. Nothing bad would have happened if he had surrendered himself or we had surrendered him."

He wanted to help her sadness, to show her at least that things might have been worse.

"You're wrong, Aunt Margaret. Something would have happened. They would have done an operation on his brain, to stop him being rebellious, to make him docile."

She looked at him, not speaking.

"It's true! Sir Percy told me. Don't you believe me? Do you think I'm lying?"

"I believe you," she said. "It is something that can't be helped. There is a scar on my husband's head; his hair hides it. It happened when he was a young man, before we were married."

He stared at her, shocked.

"No." It was he who was incredulous. "You can't mean that."

"It happens," she said. "Very rarely with girls. I suppose we are more concerned with homes and families. Not often with boys, for that matter. But it's a simple operation. There's no danger. It's not much worse than having a tooth out."

Having a tooth out . . . It was only now, listening to her quiet voice, that he realized the full horror—not just of what she was saying but of what Sir Percy had told him that morning. Mr. Gifford, watering and pruning and pinching the buds off his tiny trees, had once been like Mike, thought as he did. And they had opened his skull and nipped out the core of his manhood as he himself might nip the growing heart of a plant.

"And you would have let them take Mike, knowing what they were going to do to him?" he said.

"He would still be Mike. He would have all the things we love in him. And he would be safe and well, instead of being hunted through the fields like an animal."

"Did Mike know—about his father?"

She shook her head. "It is not a thing one talks about."

But somehow the seed of rebelliousness had been transmitted, to spring into growth when Mike found a ragged boy and helped him, and understood that someone from the Conurb could be a human being like himself. And then he had looked around and seen the stagnation and rottenness festering under the elegant surface of the life he knew: the corruption that could manipulate people like puppets, and the acquiescence of the puppets in their silken bonds.

Rob shivered. Mike had seen things to which he, almost deliberately, had blinded himself. The bait which he had been offered today and had so nearly taken had been more subtle and powerful but no less poisonous. The chance to be not a puppet, but a puppet master.

"You are young, Rob—too young to understand," Mrs. Gifford said. "But they will soon find him. I am sure they will. You cannot hide for long in the County. I told them the clothes he would be wearing, and they promised to do their best to make sure he did not get hurt."

Rob stood up.

"Are you going to bed?"

"Yes." He bowed but did not look at her. "Goodnight ma'am."

The fine weather had held and with it the moonlight. The fence glittered away in the distance, a barrier easily crossed except in men's minds. He was better equipped this time: he had brought a trowel to help him scrape a hole under the wire.

Since he made his decision a lot of things had become clear, going back even to his days in the Conurb. He remembered when he had waked in the night and heard men's voices in the Kennealys' flat. A dangerous business, one of them had said—you have to take account of the risks. He had known they were talking about his father's accident but had thought they were talking about the risks of being an electrician. But the dangerous business could have been something different. His father had been a good electrician and it was incredible he could have made the mistake he was supposed to have done. If he were part of a conspiracy, on the other hand . . . It might explain Mr. Kennealy's refusal to help when he was sent to the boarding school, too. "You'll be safer there," he had said, and then corrected it to "better looked after." Perhaps that wasn't a slip of the tongue but an expression of conviction: the son of a rebel secretly killed by the police would not be safe in the home of a fellow revolutionary.

Rob looked up at the fence. He was going back into the Conurb, back to the crowds and the smells, the processed foods and the blaring din, the mindless mob singing the latest pop song or discussing who beat whom in the Games the previous night. He was heading for the address Mike had given him. The rest was unknown and uncertain. They would be trying to create the revolution there which had failed so miserably here. Even though there might be a few who would help, like Mr. Kennealy, the odds were fantastically against them. But once you did see things clearly there was no alternative.

He remembered a long time ago, when he could only have been five or six. His father had promised to take him for a walk but canceled it at the last minute because he had to go to see Mr. Kennealy about something urgent. Rob had cried and been ashamed of crying. His father had gone all the same, and had brought him back a bar of chocolate to make amends. Rob remembered his first sulky refusal and his father's voice: "It really was important, Rob. I wouldn't have let you down for anything that wasn't important."

He had a strange feeling as though after all it had come

right. He was going with his father, long years behind but following.

Sonnet stood patiently beside him. He slapped her rump and said, "Home, girl. Back to your stable."

Then he knelt down and began to dig.